I WAS CLEOPATRA

I Was Cleopatra

Dennis Abrams

Groundwood Books
House of Anansi Press
Toronto Berkeley

The author would like to thank historian Garry Wills, whose references to John Rice in his books *Verdi's Shakespeare: Men of the Theater*, *Witches and Jesuits: Shakespeare's Macbeth* and *Making Make-Believe Real: Politics as Theater in Shakespeare's Time* inspired this work.

Published in Canada and the USA in 2018 by Groundwood Books

Groundwood Books / House of Anansi Press
groundwoodbooks.com

We acknowledge the Government of Canada for its financial support of our publishing program.

With the participation of the Government of Canada | Canadä
Avec la participation du gouvernement du Canada

Library and Archives Canada Cataloguing in Publication
Abrams, Dennis, author
    I was Cleopatra / Dennis Abrams.
Issued in print and electronic formats.
ISBN 978-1-77306-022-4 (hardcover).—ISBN 978-1-77306-023-1 (HTML).—
ISBN 978-1-77306-024-8 (Kindle)
    I. Title.
PZ7.1.A27IA 2018   J813'.6   C2017-905299-3
C2017-905300-0

Jacket art by Pablo Auladell
Jacket design by Michael Solomon

Groundwood Books is committed to protecting our natural environment. As part of our efforts, the interior of this book is printed on paper that contains 100% post-consumer recycled fibers, is acid-free and is processed chlorine-free.

Printed and bound in Canada

To Garry Wills.
And to Sheila Barry,
who believed in me, in John
and in this book.

An Introduction

In which the author lays out
the groundwork for the story
that is to come

I was Cleopatra.

I was Lady Macbeth.

I was Cordelia in Master Shakespeare's *The Tragedy of King Lear*. And I was the Fool in the same play.

I was Imogen in *Cymbeline*. I was Marina in *Pericles*. I was Paulina in *The Winter's Tale.*

I was Desdemona when England's most renowned troupe of actors, the King's Men, performed in Oxford in 1610.

I was Lucrezia Borgia in Barnabe Barnes's *The Devil's Charter.*

I was summoned to perform on numerous occasions before King James I, his family and his court.

I was featured in plays written by William Shakespeare, Ben Jonson, John Webster and other leading playwrights of my time. I knew them, worked with them, learned from them and became, I like to think, their friends.

I was, for a time, an actor at the Globe Theatre in London, where before I entered my full adulthood and because of what some called my beauty — my physical qualities and appearance and demeanor — I was featured and praised for my performances in leading women's roles, to both my shame and, I must confess, my pride.

I was loved by boys and girls and by men and women. And I loved them in return.

My name is John Rice.

I am now thirty-five years old, childless, my dear beloved wife gone for nearly ten years. She died shortly after giving birth to our son, who followed her just three days later.

The theaters are closed because the plague is once again ravaging London. The time has now come to say goodbye to all of that. The time has come for me to turn my back on that world of fakery and artifice and make-believe, and return to the real world. The time has come for me to say goodbye to the theater and, if God wills it, to find a new life and salvation in the church.

This then is a farewell to my past life.

Chapter One

In which I tell the history of
my childhood, my parents, my
brothers and sisters, and my
education

Since my life in London has been a very different one from
that of my childhood in Reading, Berkshire, and since the
life I lived in Reading is one largely unknown to the friends
and associates of my adulthood, I think it of the essence, in
order to help understand who I am, to relate in detail various aspects of that period before I came to the city.

My father, Thomas Rice, was a glover by trade, self-
made, who earned a fair living manufacturing and selling
gloves and other leather goods to the town's gentry as well
as to those of our own merçantile class.

My mother, Jane, was of a good and godly family from
the nearby countryside, and gave to my father seven children. The first of them was my elder brother, Thomas, my
hero and also rival for our father's affection, born in 1588.

Following were myself, born in 1590; my brother William, born a year later but taken by the plague at the age of two; my beloved sister Elizabeth, born in 1593, who despite being three years my younger seemed to understand me the best; my brother Edward, born one year later, taken by smallpox at the age of six; my sister Agnes, born in 1596 but taken by measles before she was a year old; and my youngest brother, Henry, born in 1597, at the same moment my mother died giving him birth.

Because of our father's success as a glove maker and merchant, and due to the everlasting grace of God, our lives were comfortable, at least compared to others I saw in town, and, in particular, compared to those unfortunate poor I would see every day of my time in London.

Our house was built in the old style that can still be found in the further reaches of the country. There were two stories, with a hall and parlor on the ground floor, both with hearths that provided warmth for the rest of the house. The upstairs was one large room where all slept — Father and Mother in the best bed, my brothers and I in one of lesser quality but still elevated off the ground in a wooden frame and stuffed with the sweetest-smelling barley straw available. My sister slept in a similar bed, and our servant slept in the corner of the room in a coarsely stuffed straw bed set directly on the ground.

The kitchen was in the back, in a small building separate from the main house. Alongside it were the brew house, where my mother made our daily beer and ale, a small apiary that provided enough honey for the family as well as some additional for my mother to sell at the market held each Wednesday, and a small vegetable and herb garden.

Father's workshop was in a room added on to the house, across from the main hall. There, with the gloves, belts, purses and aprons that he crafted with the aid of his assistants, were kept the animal skins used in their making. The house was filled with the pungent aroma of the family's urine, collected every morning from the chamber pots kept under our beds and used to soften the skins. Less pungent but equally memorable were the yeasty aromas of brewing beer and our daily bread baking that wafted in from the outside.

My childhood was a childhood like any other with one exception perhaps worthy of mention. My brother Thomas was strong and healthy and adept at what boys were expected to be good at, and so was, quite naturally, the favorite of my father's eye. I was not so strong and healthy. I was small and thin, not at all good at archery and other physical activities that I was expected to be good at. Added to that, and perhaps increasing the shame I felt my father had at having a son such as myself, I was, in the words of our servant Mary, "pretty enough in himself to be a girl." To this sentiment my mother nodded her quiet assent, and perhaps out of sympathy, she allowed me extra attention and encouragement.

Although she never learned to write anything beyond her own name, Mother did know how to read. So it was she who patiently taught me and my brothers and sisters the letters of the alphabet, the rudiments of reading and, of course, our morning and evening prayers, which she, in particular, loved to hear me sing. She would often tell me her wish for me was that I would, when the time came, enter the church and live a life of quiet devotion to our Lord and Savior.

Thanks to Mother's encouragement, I took to my lessons well, which is why, in part, her death was such a great loss for me. After she passed (and I can still hear her screams of pain before the sudden silence of her death was quickly filled in with the cries of newly born Henry), I felt very much alone.

And so two years later, while Thomas remained at home to learn the glovers' trade, which I was quite obviously not meant for (since lifting the heavy hides, treating them, cutting them — all the physical effort needed was beyond my abilities), at the age of nine, I was taken out of my child-hood gown, put into my first adult pants and linen shirt, and sent off to the local primary school. There I continued my education, in the hope that it would help me to eventually find a trade.

The primary school my father sent me to, named after King Edward VI, was much the same as any other in the region. There were fifteen boys in attendance, with a screen dividing the room between the younger boys and those who were older and more advanced.

My day started early. I rose at five, said my prayers, cleansed my face and then, tucking the tail of my shirt between my legs as was the custom, put on my pants, had a small breakfast of bread and fruit and ale, and went off to school.

Class began at six during the summer, but during the winter months, when early light was scarce, it began as late as seven. For the next four years I attended school. During my first two years, mornings were spent studying Latin grammar, and then once grammar was mastered, in study-ing and memorizing the classic Latin texts. I was allowed to go home for thirty minutes at midday for my dinner, then returned to school for afternoon classes until just before dark, with more Latin to be memorized, additional Latin to be recited, and Latin to be discussed and argued over.

Our first textbook, Lily's *A Short Introduction to Grammar*, which, truth be told, was not in its essence short in the least, was used to lay the groundwork for all the lessons that were to come. The next step in our education was practicing conversation and then letter writing — learning how to say "thank you for your letter" in one hundred and fifty different ways, or perhaps pretending that I was Julius Caesar writing a letter to the Roman Senate requesting that they grant him power and responsibilities beyond those he already had.

In order to instruct us thoroughly, the master would read us a text in Latin, declare its argument by suggesting a motto or some other way to summarize it and thus fit it into our memories, then translate it into English, carefully explaining and analyzing the grammar, both in Latin and in English, as he went along. Tests of our ability to translate and to memorize the texts were given each day, and any errors or mistakes or hesitations when being questioned were dealt with sternly.

But after those skills were mastered, we were, to my delight if not always that of my schoolmates, introduced to classical literature: Ovid and his tales of magic and metamorphoses, Aesop and his fables, Virgil, Cicero and so many others. The many hours spent learning these stories and memorizing long passages of poetry and prose to the satisfaction of my teacher proved to be invaluable to me in my future life on the stage.

I was most fortunate in that my schoolteacher, Master Harding, was sympathetic to his young charges and didn't berate or beat us more than was necessary and deserved. Latin seemed to come easily to me, and while my schoolmates often teased and mocked me for what they termed my "girlish" ways and lack of interest in their rough-and-tumble manner of play, they were, most thankfully, largely silent when it came to my school work.

And while I hesitate to appear or to sound boastful or prideful, I excelled when we were called upon to read and perform plays written by the ancient masters, in particular the comedies of Terence and Plautus. I was, again, because of my small stature and more feminine way of being (at least when compared to some of the other boys), called upon to play the female leads in those plays.

And here, I must confess, I felt a singular kind of liberation. In performing the role of a young girl, I was, although in part embarrassed, also oddly comfortable, embracing qualities in myself that in everyday life were to be mocked and scorned, but in the schoolroom setting generated praise from Master Harding that brought me deep satisfaction.

So it was in this way that my life as a young boy proceeded along its prescribed path of school, family, births, deaths and the passage of the seasons, until the year 1603, when at the age of thirteen I found myself on an entirely new road.

Chapter Two

In which I describe the means
by which I became an actor

The time had come for my father to decide in what manner
I would earn my living and how to arrange for my training, since, as was apparent to all including myself, I was
not made in such a way as to allow me to work as a glover
alongside him and my brother.

In 1603 the plague once again struck London with a
terrible ferocity, bringing about the deaths of thousands
of innocent men, women and children. To help stop the
spread of the dreaded disease, which at its height was laying more than thirteen hundred innocents dead from one
Sabbath to the next, it was ordered that theaters in London
be closed. It was the combination of those two events, fortunate and unfortunate, that led to my life on the stage.

Being unable to perform and earn a living in London,
the King's Men, the city's most praised and renowned group
of actors, escaped the pestilence by touring the provinces

and performing some of their most popular productions in front of audiences who would not have had the chance to see them otherwise. And so, by the grace of God, they came to Reading.

Encouraged to do so by Master Harding, my father obtained tickets for us to attend a performance of Master Shakespeare's comedy *As You Like It*. Reading, with the exception of a few Puritans who rejected the notion of staged theatrics on religious grounds, was in a state of excitement unmatched by even the yearly fair.

The weather was fine on the warm late fall afternoon that the King's Men performed, and as my father and I stood below the level of the stage (erected especially on the occasion of the players' visit), I found myself enthralled by what I was seeing and hearing, as well as overcome with emotions that were altogether unfamiliar to me.

Alexander Cook, then eighteen years old and nearing the end of his successful career acting in women's roles, played the delightful heroine Rosalind. I stood gape-jawed in amazement and wonder as Alexander, who would later prove to be a good friend and more, transformed himself into Rosalind, and then when Rosalind slipped into her disguise as the young man Ganymede, magically became a man playing a woman playing a man. I was in raptures, not only from the play itself and the spell cast by Alexander, but also from the reaction of the crowd, willing itself to believe that Alexander was actually a young woman pretending to be a man and not the young man he really was, with the first faint wisps of a beard to prove it.

As magical as it all was, the moment that I shall never forget — the moment that seemed to change something within me — came at the end of the production, with the play's epilogue. Alexander, still in costume as Rosalind, came onstage one last time to address the audience. I can still remember his final words:

> If I were a woman I would kiss as many of you as had beards that pleased me, complexions that liked me and breaths that I defied not. And I am sure as many as have good beards, or good faces, or sweet breaths will for my kind offer, when I make curtsy, bid me farewell.

I confess that I knew not what to think. There he was, a young man dressed as a woman who had disguised herself as a man before returning to womanhood again, promising to kiss the men in the audience, somehow and in some way straddling a line between man and woman that frightened me, excited me and stirred something in me that I did not and perhaps still do not understand.

My father, standing next to me, had been watching me and my reaction to the play for the entirety of the performance. After it was over, he took me by the hand and led me back to where the company had assembled, pushing against the crowd to do so. He then abruptly thrust me in front of the troupe's manager and sometimes actor, John Heminges.

"This is my boy, John Rice," he gruffly told the silent Heminges. "I'd like to apprentice him to you, since it seems clear to me now that this is the life he was meant for. He's not meant to be a tanner, of that I am certain."

Whether Father honestly believed that what he was doing was the best for me, or whether he was relieved to find a way to send his disappointment of a son out of his sight is a question I've never resolved to my own satisfaction.

Heminges, who I would come to know quite well as a master and teacher and ultimately as a friend, looked me up and down. My appearance was clearly pleasing to him, and he spoke gently and kindly to me, asking me questions about myself and my schooling. He allowed himself a small smile when he heard me speak, my voice still as high-pitched as that of any girl. After hearing me sing a hymn and recite a portion of one of Virgil's eclogues, he turned to my father, telling him that since the time had come for Alexander to begin moving from women's to men's roles, he and the company were in need of a young boy such as myself to hopefully, if my talent so allowed, take his place.

While he and my father stepped away to discuss the details of my future career, the cost of my apprenticeship, and, indeed, whether I should be accepted as his apprentice at all, I looked around at the group of actors, excited and nervous. All thoughts of my mother's wish for me vanished. Instead, I found myself hoping beyond hope that my future would be with them, for they and the life they had seemed to offer me a way of escaping my home and becoming what I knew, beyond a moment's doubt, I wanted to be and was meant to be.

I felt my heart beat faster and faster and my breath come more and more quickly as each moment passed, and I prayed to be granted the first thing I had ever truly wanted for myself. My eyes caught those of Alexander, who, perhaps sensing my fear and hope and need to be accepted as a member of the troupe, smiled at me encouragingly, seeming with one glance to understand and accept who I was.

Several minutes later, my father returned, placed his hand on my shoulder and announced to me that I would be joining the King's Men as an apprentice, that I was to honor my master and learn the acting trade to the best of my abilities, while continuing to be a good and dutiful son and an obedient servant of God.

Three days later, along with what few belongings I possessed, I left my home with the King's Men, joining with them for the remainder of their tour, then onward to London and whatever my future might bring.

Chapter Three

In which I describe my first
impressions of my new master,
the actor John Heminges, and
my time on the road with the
King's Men

When I left home, I was but thirteen years old and had never
before been more than a mile or two away from Reading. I
had never before spent a night away from my father and
brothers and sisters, and yet here I was walking away from
them with a troupe of actors whom I had never before known,
going towards a future life I could not yet begin to imagine.

I here admit that on that first night as I lay curled up
in the cart in which we slept, missing my father and sib-
lings and home and all that I knew and felt familiar with,
my fears and worries and feeling of being alone got the best
of me, and much to my shame I began to cry. Alexander,
who was still awake and talking with his friends, came over
and lay directly next to me and did his best to comfort me

by gently stroking my hair and back, while softly singing a song he told me he had heard Master Heminges's wife sing to her children:

> Golden slumbers kiss your eyes,
> Smiles awake you when you rise.
> Sleep, pretty wantons, do not cry,
> And I will sing a lullaby:
> Rock them, rock them, lullaby.
>
> Care is heavy, therefore sleep you;
> You are care, and care must keep you.
> Sleep, pretty wantons, do not cry,
> And I will sing a lullaby:
> Rock them, rock them, lullaby.

As he half-sang, half-whispered the lyrics into my ear, I felt myself comforted and not nearly so alone, and I quickly fell asleep.

The next morning, the other actors looked at me with an initial curiosity, which soon changed to a seeming and apparent disinterest. I quickly came to realize that I would largely be ignored until I proved myself worthy of being in their company.

I was fortunate though in that my master, John Heminges, took pity on my feelings of loss and isolation, and walked alongside me for a good deal of our travels over the next several weeks, asking me about myself and telling me about his own life as an actor and shareholder in the Globe Theatre.

Thirty-seven years of age when he took me on as his apprentice, Master Heminges had nearly completed his own apprenticeship as a grocer when, in 1588, he married Rebecca Knell, the sixteen-year-old widow of William Knell, who had been a member of the acting troupe known as the Queen's Men. Working as a grocer did not and could not, he swore to me, compare to life in the theater, and within the course of just six years, he had established himself as a lead actor with Lord Strange's Men and three years later found himself as one of the Chamberlain's Men, the troupe of actors and playwrights supported and licensed to perform by Henry Carey, the Lord Chamberlain. That same troupe, just two months before I was apprenticed to it, became known as the King's Men, serving under the patronage of His Royal Highness, the newly crowned James I.

It was that patronage, I learned, that allowed us (and I am making free use of the word "us," as I was not as of yet an 'official member of the troupe) to legally perform plays on stage at the Globe as well as while touring the country. It also gave playwright Master Shakespeare the title of "Groom of the Chamber" and rewarded him and the other shareholders four and a half yards of red cloth each for royal livery, to be worn only on state occasions.

I was immersed immediately into the acting life during those weeks on the road, as we awaited news that the plague had ended in London and the theaters had been reopened. We traveled from town to town, largely on foot, one wagon piled high with the company's possessions and costumes, pulled by an exhausted-looking horse that Richard III himself would have questioned giving up his kingdom for. I was informed, during the course of our travels, that this tour was successful, at least in comparison to a similar one a decade earlier when the theaters in London had closed due to the plague, and the troupe had toured the countryside with so little success that everything, including costumes and props, had to be sold in order for the actors to eat.

When we arrived in a likely-looking place, be it a larger city such as Bath or Shrewsbury, or one of the smaller towns in between, Master Heminges would change out of his dusty travel clothes and into his most elaborate regal-looking costume. He would then present our papers to the town's officials and ceremonially request permission to perform that evening. When permission was granted, and it was rare that it was not, the first task given to me as an apprentice was to act as the troupe's public crier, walking through the town announcing that the King's Men had arrived direct from London to perform the exact same plays presented to the royal court. I would shout out (or sing out in all truth, given my still high-pitched voice) the name of the production being performed.

On the first day it was generally the play I saw performed in Berkshire, Shakespeare's *As You Like It*. If we stayed a second evening, *The Tragedy of Hamlet* would be performed. If a third night was called for, it would be either *The Life of King Henry the Fifth* or *A Warning for Fair Women*, the choice dependent on what Master Heminges and the other senior members of the troupe determined would be a more popular choice, given the demeanor of the previous afternoon's audience.

At this point I was not yet allowed on the stage. I was under instructions from Master Heminges to observe everything, to learn as much as was possible on how the actors performed, how they moved, how they projected their words, and most of all to absorb everything done on stage by

Alexander, both in his role as Rosalind in *As You Like It* and as the most piteous and heartbreaking Ophelia imaginable in *Hamlet*.

I had shared a few words with Alexander by this point and found him supportive of me and willing to assist me in any way possible. He said he was most eager to move on from women's to men's roles. In my youth and naivety, I trusted in him when he told me this. I was later to learn that this was to some degree an act of bravado on Alexander's part, since actors are always acting. The transition from playing women's roles to men's was often a difficult one, and many a boy actor's career ended when he was able to grow his first beard.

And that was exactly the age that Alexander was. If one looked carefully, the first thin wisps of facial hair were apparent, and while Alexander was rightly proud of them, he also, at the same time, did whatever was possible to cover them up and keep them hidden from view.

While Alexander might rightly have been concerned about his future, one could not see it in his performance. I'd seen his Rosalind and knew what to expect, but I was again positively bewitched by the ease with which the young man I was coming to know as a potential friend transformed himself into Rosalind, and then Ganymede when she flees for her life into the Forest of Arden.

But I was even more transfixed by his transformation into the young girl Ophelia in Master Shakespeare's *Hamlet*, which he enacted at Oxford in one of the college halls. A character most dissimilar to the bold and courageous Rosalind, Ophelia, whose love for the young Hamlet is ultimately dismissed by him with a rage-filled scorn, lacks Rosalind's strength and by play's end dissolves into madness, and then, ultimately and most regrettably, suicide. I shall never as long as I live forget Alexander's portrait of Ophelia's fragility, and then the good Queen Gertrude's mournful response to her tragic end, which to my eyes and ears seemed the perfect response to Alexander's delicate portrayal:

> Her clothes spread wide,
> And mermaid-like awhile they bore her up,
> Which time she chanted snatches of old lauds,
> As one incapable of her own distress,
> Or like a creature native and indued
> Unto that element. But long it could not be
> 'Till that her garments, heavy with their drink,
> Pull'd the poor wretch from her melodious lay
> To muddy death.

Many years later, when I was awarded the opportunity to perform the role of Gertrude, I recalled the image of my dear lovely Alexander as Ophelia, lying drowned in the weeping brook, as I recited those lines. Real tears came into my eyes as I did so.

We had been touring the countryside for three or more weeks when word reached us in October that the plague had, God be praised, seemingly run its course, and the theaters had been given permission to reopen. With that, we immediately set forth for London, where my real apprenticeship would at last begin.

Chapter Four

In which I describe our
entrance into London, my
initial impressions of the great
city, and my introduction
to the Globe and to Master
Shakespeare

It was difficult for me to fully comprehend. For the first time in my life, I, John Rice of Reading, was approaching the great city of London in the company of the King's Men to which I was now apprenticed, walking arm in arm with my new friend and protector, Alexander, when less than a month prior, I had been nothing more than a lonely schoolboy.

While I have lived in London for a goodly number of years now, and its wonders have become routine, I still shall never forget my first walk into the city. We had changed into our theatrical costumes — even I, although still in the garb of a young boy — and we waved banners and beat drums to allow the city's residents to know that we had returned from the road and that our theater, the Globe, would once again be open to welcome audiences.

We entered into the city at St. Magnus's Corner on the northern end of the great London Bridge. It was a sight unlike any I had ever before seen. The roadway was crowded with more people assembled in one place than I could have possibly imagined. The road was held up over the river by heavy stone piers, and on either side were houses as well as shops selling luxury items of the very highest quality. Indeed, as Alexander pointed out to me, there was right on the bridge a store selling meats and produce of all kinds, housed in an ancient two-story-tall stone building.

I began to feel more and more anxious as the crowds grew even thicker, and I held tight to Alexander for fear of getting separated and lost in a city I had no knowledge of. We had nearly crossed the bridge when I saw them. There, on the Great Stone Gate, nearly at the Southwark side of the bridge, were severed heads, what seemed to be thirty of them in total, stuck on poles for all to see. There were so many that, as I later learned, they necessitated the employment of an official Keeper of the Heads. On some the flesh had completely rotted away, leaving nothing but the gaping stare of the skulls. Other heads still had pieces of skin attached to them and were surrounded by swarms of buzzing flies. On one a lone black crow sat vigil, staring blankly ahead, idly picking at what remained of the dead person's scalp.

I remember staring at them in horror, unable to move, amazed that the crowds were able to walk past as though they were nothing out of the ordinary. Alexander gently pulled me along off the bridge, and I realized once we were past that my entire body was shivering with fright. I felt my friend put his arm around my shoulders and tell me that I was not to be afraid, that they were the heads of those who had conspired against the king, traitors who deserved their fate, whose remains were placed there for all to see as a warning.

The rest of the walk was a blur, a mixture of sounds and sights and smells that melded together into a swirl of impressions that remain with me yet all these years later. The sounds of the workmen and their tools, the sing-song chanting of the women walking down the road selling their wares — "Hot pies of all sorts, mutton pies, leek pies, kidney pies … sausage … buy my glasses … bay and rosemary for remembrance …" — blended with the sounds of the milk-maids, the merchants calling out for customers, the bellowing of the cattle and grunts of the swine being driven to market … a mix of such distinction that I can close my eyes and the scene is there before me, as vivid as it was when I arrived that first day in London.

Alexander seemed bemused at how rapidly my mood had changed. The fear and repulsion I had felt on the bridge encountering the piked heads of traitors had disappeared, to be replaced with a growing sense of excitement along with something approaching awe. This, I thought, is what life is like, what life should be like. This, I thought, is where life is, not in the quiet of the countryside but here in the city, where, it seemed, anything and everything could be found, where everything was possible. These feelings only deepened my resolve to succeed in the theater. Less than an hour after entering the great world that is London, I knew that no matter what, this would be my home.

But while London would be and still remains my home, my physical home for the time of my apprenticeship was to be with Master Heminges. He, along with his wife, Rebecca, and their five surviving children (four had not survived infancy, another four would arrive during the time of my apprenticeship) lived in a somewhat crowded home in the parish of St. Mary, Aldermanbury. Their home, I was to learn later, was a less-than-ten-minute walk from the residence on Silver Street where Master Shakespeare lodged with his friends the Montjoys.

Also living with my master was my new friend, Alexander, who would remain there until his life abruptly changed and his apprenticeship came to an end. For the time being though, we would be bedmates, sharing a small bed on the upper level of Heminges's house where we would often, on cold nights, lie pressed together for warmth. During those nights, as we became more familiar with each other, Alexander would tell me about his life, about the theater and acting, while giving me what would prove to be invaluable lessons on the art of personation — how to transform myself from the young boy I was into the young girl or woman that the parts I would play required.

But that was still to come. The next morning, after quickly eating a slab of bread and cheese at a long table shared with the entire family, Master Heminges, Alexander and myself crossed the river over to Southwark and the place that would become the center of my existence, the place where I discovered what I was capable of being, the place where I was made much of and felt myself to be at last myself — the Globe Theatre.

That theater is gone now, burned to the ground during

a performance of Master Shakespeare's *The Famous History of the Life of King Henry the Eighth*, or as it was more commonly known, *All Is True*. And while it is also true that the theater was rebuilt, the new one never quite, as I see it, captured the magic of the original.

The Globe, along with the Swan and Rose theaters, was located in Southwark, which although just across the Thames from the city proper, was not then under the jurisdiction of the city authorities. For this reason the area was filled with entertainments of all sorts not necessarily thought moral and proper. Along with theatrical productions, visitors to the area could avail themselves of establishments where dancing was allowed, where prostitutes of all sorts plied their trade, where entertainments of the most brutish kinds were presented to crowds who exulted in sports that were, in truth, celebrations of blood and death.

I shall talk about those kinds of entertainments at greater length later in this memoir, but now I'd prefer to remember instead the first Globe Theatre and the story of its construction, or actually its reconstruction in 1599, which it seems likely few now remember.

It was Master Heminges who told me of its history. In the year of our Lord 1576, James Burbage had built the first building in London dedicated solely to theatrical performances, known simply as "The Theatre," which became the home of the Lord Chamberlain's Men. It was here that the early works of Master Shakespeare were performed, as well as those of Christopher Marlowe and Thomas Kyd, the popularity of whose play *The Spanish Tragedy*, now I believe seldom performed, helped the playhouse to remain profitable even during the leanest of times.

Even though the Theatre was successful, as the year of our Lord 1598 came to a close, James Burbage and his son Richard Burbage, the lead actor with what was then the Lord Chamberlain's Men, now the King's Men, came to learn that the owner of the land on which the Theatre had been built had plans to tear it down. But before that could happen, James's brother Cuthbert found a new site on which to build, in Southwark, close to St. Saviour's church, south of Maiden Lane and west of Dead Man's Lane.

And so on the 28th of December of that year, the Burbage brothers, along with players from the Lord Chamberlain's Men as well as any other able-bodied souls who could be persuaded to help, dismantled the Theatre piece by piece, then transported the timber to Peter Street's Wharf at Bridewell Stairs. There it was loaded onto barges in the dark of night, sailed across the Thames at high tide and then brought forth to Dead Man's Place, where it sat until the beginning of the new year and the work of reconstruction could begin.

By the time my master had related the history of the Globe, we had approached it. To my surprise, the theater itself, despite its name, was not strictly round like a globe. Instead, by my count, it was a twenty-sided edifice. Close by the entrance, a flag depicted Hercules carrying the globe on his back, much as the players had done with the Globe, along with the Latin words *totus mundus agit histrionem*, meaning "the whole world is a playhouse." (Although the flag only flew on the days the King's Men performed, on this day, their first day back in the theater in months, it was felt appropriate to fly it as an announcement that the theaters were open once again.)

On entering, my first time ever inside a theater, I saw a stage of a rectangular shape, approximately five feet in height, which jutted out halfway into the yard where those who stood for the performance would surround it. Along the wall were two circular galleries with seats for those with the means to pay for them, where they were protected from the elements under a thick thatched roof. I could smell the straw covering the floor, the scent of sweat and beer and something I did not yet recognize but grew to know as the makeup of the actors, still lingering from the last performances before the theater had been shut down.

The stage itself was also covered by a thatched gable and an attached roof made of oak. There was a beautiful ceiling rightly called "the heavens," painted a bold midnight blue, divided into sections adorned with stars, the sun, the moon and all the signs of the zodiac. Above the balcony where the musicians would play were images of the ancient gods Mercury and Apollo, as well as the muses of comedy and tragedy.

While Master Heminges and Alexander talked with two of the other players, I clambered up on the stage to get a closer look at all the glory painted above, then turned around to face where the audience would be. As I stood, imagining what it might be like to receive the approval of the crowd and feeling my heart begin to race at the prospect, I heard a friendly voice behind me.

"So, John Heminges … is this your new boy?"

It was Master William Shakespeare, the King's Men's leading playwright, and one whose faith and trust in my limited talent allowed me the opportunity to perform the finest roles of my time in the theater.

Chapter Five

In which I perform for Master
Shakespeare, he offers me
advice on acting, and my
lessons begin

He was a man then approaching forty, still hale and healthy,
dressed in clothing suiting his station in life. His shirt was
of a good quality, although not the best material; the doublet covering it was new and showed his worthiness to be
under the employ of His Majesty, James I. But I must add,
the hose that covered him from his waist down and the
lace ruff around his neck both seemed to have been chosen
carelessly or haphazardly, since they displayed signs of wear
not evident in his other garments. His hair appeared to be
hastily combed, although his beard was well groomed. His
fingers and the cuffs of his shirt were, as befitted a writer,
stained with splotches of ink.

As I saw when I turned to the rear of the stage, his face
appeared kindly, with a look of amusement at what he must

have seen as my eagerness to accept my first applause.

"He impresses me as being a likely one," he told Heminges, "but does his voice match his outward appearance?"

And so began my first testing by Master Shakespeare. He asked first to hear me sing and so I did, nervously recalling the lyrics to "Greensleeves," a song my mother often sang to me and my brothers and sisters:

> Alas, my love, you do me wrong,
> To cast me off discourteously.
> And I have loved you oh so long,
> Delighting in your company.
>
> Greensleeves was all my joy,
> Greensleeves was my delight,
> Greensleeves was my heart of gold.
> And who but my lady greensleeves.

As I sang, I espied the two gentlemen exchanging apparent looks of approval, which gave me the confidence, after Shakespeare asked to hear another, to sing for them the madrigal "Flow My Tears," composed by John Dowland. It was a song that never failed to move me deeply, whether I heard it sung by another or when, feeling sorry for myself, I sang it softly to myself alone.

> Flow, my tears, fall from your springs!
> Exiled for ever, let me mourn;
> Where night's black bird her sad infamy sings,
> There let me live forlorn.

Down vain lights, shine you no more!
No nights are dark enough for those
That in despair their last fortunes deplore.
Light doth but shame disclose.

Never may my woes be relieved,
Since pity is fled;
And tears and sighs and groans my weary days,
    my weary days
Of all joys have deprived.

I confess singing those lyrics brought me nearly to tears as I recalled the feelings of loneliness I had often felt in the house of my parents, as well as the deep pain that still lingered from the loss of my mother. And so when I looked to see the reaction of Masters Shakespeare and Heminges and saw what appeared to be tears welling in the eyes of both honorable gentlemen, I felt a sudden and unexpected rush of pride that my song had had such an impact.

The two once again exchanged glances of whose meaning I could not quite grasp. Shakespeare then looked through his doublet until he found the paper he was seeking and then gave it over to me.

"This," he told me, "is from my play *The Tragedy of Romeo and Juliet*. In this scene, the young girl Juliet is standing on a balcony outside her bedroom. Earlier that evening, she has met and immediately fallen in love with a young man named Romeo, and she is now proclaiming her love for him. Please, if you will, read this over once, ask of me any questions you might have, and then read it as if you were, as you stand here, a young girl in love for the first time."

I was now at a loss. I had never been in love. I had, most obviously, never been a young girl in love. How was I to know how she would say it? But as I read over the short scene, I envisioned myself as a young girl standing on the balcony, looking down at Romeo who had, in but a moment, stirred within me my first feelings of love. And then when Shakespeare called over Alexander to read Romeo's lines in response to mine, who Juliet was and what she felt became clear and understandable.

I started, stuttered, heard Shakespeare ask me encouragingly to begin again, and read:

JULIET
Good night, good night; as sweet repose and rest
Come to thy heart as that within my breast.

ROMEO
O, wilt thou leave me so unsatisfied?

JULIET
What satisfaction canst thou have to-night?

ROMEO
The exchange of thy love's faithful vow for mine.

JULIET
I gave thee mine before thou didst request it,
And yet I would it were to give again.

ROMEO
Wouldst thou withdraw it? For what purpose, love?

JULIET
But to be frank, and give it thee again.
And yet I wish but for the thing I have:
My bounty is as boundless as the sea,
My love as deep; the more I give to thee,
The more I have, for both are infinite.

I was breathless as we ended the scene. I had for a moment, for just a brief moment, in an odd way become Juliet as I declared to Alexander that "My bounty is as boundless as the sea, / My love as deep; the more I give to thee, / The more I have, for both are infinite." For his part, Alexander was looking at me with a strange expression I had never seen him wear before.

To my pleasure, the man who had written the words simply told me, "Well done, John," and then added, "I must take your leave now, but you are in good hands with Heminges here. There is little he and the others cannot teach you about the art of acting. I do though want to give you the following advice. When reading, speak the speech trippingly on the tongue, but do not saw the air too much your hand, rather use it gently. Suit the action to the words you are speaking, and the words to the action. Your task, as I see it, young John, is to hold the mirror up to nature herself. And with those words, I leave you. Think upon them, and listen to all that your master has to say. I shall see you anon."

With that, Master Shakespeare left the theater, leaving me to work with the rest of the players, all of whom were preparing for their first performance at the Globe since the theaters had been reopened. The play, *The Merry Devil of*

Edmonton, had been a success the previous year and was viewed as likely to fill the company coffers quickly before winter set in and the theater would once again be forced to close its doors.

I watched silently, dining on the bread and ale Mistress Heminges had packed for Alexander and myself, while the bookkeeper assigned each of the players their roles. As was generally the case, Richard Burbage, a fine-looking gentleman with a high forehead and a sad, haunted look in his eyes, was given the leading role. Alexander was given the primary female role, and the remaining roles were given to the other players depending on their type. Two to three parts were given to each of the actors with minor roles, making it possible for our small company to present plays with casts of characters far exceeding our usual ten permanent players.

As it was late afternoon and the theater was already darkening, the other players left and returned to their homes. There would be a quick rehearsal the next morning, finishing in time for the actors to get into costumes and makeup and prepare for the afternoon performance heralded by the tolling of the bells from nearby Southwark Cathedral.

Before leaving to return home, Alexander took me about the theater and described to me the skills I would of necessity have to learn in order to perform as a woman: I would need to be able to dance skillfully, to sing like a nightingale, to speak my lines truthfully and eloquently, and to learn to memorize a great number of lines in an exceedingly short period of time. Perhaps most essential, I would need to learn to walk, to sit, to use hand gestures, and indeed my entire body, with such grace as to become a convincing woman on stage.

I would, he told me, have to learn to display to the audience a certain softness. I would have to perform with an air of feminine sweetness in my every moment on the stage, remembering always that while men and women do share some common qualities, a woman should not resemble a man when it came to her manners, words, gestures and bearing. And that while it was altogether fitting that a man should display a robust and sturdy air of manliness (and here he gave me an odd little smile), a woman, whether in real life or as portrayed on stage, should always have a certain delicate tenderness.

When I enquired to him as to whether these skills were difficult to learn, he assured me that they were not. And that just as he had learned them from the actor he later replaced, so I would from him, as well as with assistance from the other King's Men.

As we left to walk through the crowds of Southwark, he told me that I was not to worry, that my reading with him of Juliet had demonstrated that I could speak the lines as well as anyone could possibly hope for, and that he would do everything he could to teach me all that was necessary to become a woman on stage. And so as we walked through the crowded streets, his arm around my shoulders, both to protect me from the crowd as well as to show me his feelings of warmth and friendship, I felt utterly safe and assured that I would be able to do all that was asked of me.

Chapter Six

In which I describe
my training

It would still be several months before I was to appear on stage. Indeed, it would be several months until the King's Men were able to perform onstage at all, since the news we had received that the theaters had been allowed to reopen to the public, based on letters that had circulated among the city's various theatrical groups saying that all the companies could "safely home to their theaters and to their own homes," proved to be false.

During this time, the majority of the King's Men retreated to the nearby suburb of Mortlake, returning when they could to perform at the homes of various members of the gentry and aristocracy in and around the city, although using few actors due to the smaller stage spaces available. But despite the monies earned for those performances, until the commencement of the Christmas-Candlemas season (those forty days in which we celebrate the birth of our Lord

Jesus Christ) our financial well-being would be dependent on the goodwill of our royal patron. In his generosity, he sent Master Burbage a payment (or so I was informed) of thirty pounds for the maintenance and preservation of the company, since the still-too-high number of cases of the plague forced the theaters in London to remain closed.

And so it was during the month of November and the first half of December that I was given the opportunity to take lessons with the members of the troupe — to learn how to walk properly, to sit and to use hand gestures in the way that a gentlewoman would do so.

Gestures were taught to me by Alexander and other actors. I learned that the hand speaks all languages in a manner that is generally understood by all, even when spoken languages differ one to the other. I practiced and practiced and practiced, attempting to add to the gesture by thinking hard about the feelings and emotion behind it, trying to personate the emotion in question, whether it be happiness, sadness or despair.

Not only was it required that I learn how to use my hands and to move my body as a woman would, I also had to learn how to use a sword and to sing, which was a talent that seemed to be a part of my very nature. But there was also dancing, which I found the most difficult skill of all to master.

I was taken to a dancing school to learn the two basic forms of dance: basse dance, or the measure, in which case my feet were not to ever leave the ground, and the haute dance, which did require my feet to leave the ground through a combination of hopping, leaping and high jumps. I did well enough on the measure, but my strength and coordination faltered when it came to the haute dance. Many a

time I would falter, slip and fall to the ground to the obvious
dismay of the dancing master, who would lose his temper,
strike me and demand that I repeat the movement. Eventually, through hours of practice tempered with a strong fear
of being struck again, I learned the steps well enough, if
not approaching the level of grace Master Heminges and I
would have preferred me to have.

I was so eager to learn all that I could about theater
and drama and acting that I spent a portion of the small
allowance granted to me by Master Heminges to go to
the bookstalls hidden away in the churchyard of St. Paul's
Cathedral. There I purchased inexpensive cheaply printed
copies of some of the works of Masters Shakespeare and Ben
Jonson that had earlier been staged at the Theatre and at the
Globe, along with others that caught my eye and interest. I
would read them hungrily, imagining myself performing in
them, and even sometimes, I admit shamefacedly, reading
the lines of the woman's part aloud while gesturing wildly,
often without my realizing I was doing so.

On one such occasion, I recall, I was reading aloud the
lines said by Beatrice in Master Shakespeare's *Much Ado
About Nothing* in which, ironically enough given my lack
of natural talent for the art, the character speaks about the
styles of dance and how they would be learned:

> The fault will be with the music, cousin, if you be not
> wooed in good time. If the prince be too important,
> tell him there is a measure in everything, and so
> dance out the answer. For hear me, Hero, wooing,
> wedding and repenting is a Scotch jig, a measure,
> and cinque pace. The first suit is hot and hasty, like

a Scotch jig, and full as fantastical; the wedding man-
nerly modest, as a measure full of state and ancientry;
And then comes Repentance, and with his bad legs
falls into the cinque pace faster and faster till he sinks
in his grave …

I was reading these lines with what I thought were the
appropriate movements and gestures, and just as I was
sinking into my grave, I heard a cough — it was Master
Shakespeare himself!

"Steady yourself, young John," he told me with the slightest of twinkles in his eyes. "I've heard that you are learning
rapidly, and that is fine," he said. "You're not quite ready
yet for a role such as Beatrice though … but not to worry, I
know you will be. And very soon at that." And then, he left
me, standing red-faced and yet hopeful that the time would
come. And very soon.

The more time I spent with Alexander and the more
he told me about his career on stage, about the attention
paid to him, about the feeling one gets at the end of a performance receiving the approval of the crowd, the more I
wanted it for myself. I felt within me the stirring of a strong
desire for approval — from Alexander, from the King's
Men, from Master Heminges and Master Shakespeare, and
finally, from an audience. I had yet to step onto a stage and
perform, but to my astonishment, my ambitions were growing by leaps and bounds.

And as our friendship grew, so too did Alexander's encouragement of my ambitions. He seemed to take a special interest
in me, not only as someone who was responsible, at least in
part, to provide me with the training necessary to assume his

role as an actor of women's parts, but also in other ways —
ways in which I did not, during that period, quite understand.

He would tell me stories about the other writers he had
met, including Kit Marlowe, whose death in a tavern fight
several years earlier still inspired whispered rumors, and
whose scandalous reputation had besmirched his name as
a poet and playwright known for the beauty of his verse.
One day, Alexander shyly presented me for the first time
with a gift — a copy of Marlowe's poem "Hero and Leander."
The poem retells the mythical love story of Hero, a priestess
dedicated to the goddess of love, Venus, and the beautiful
boy named Leander.

What I found shocking while at the same time exciting
was Marlowe's portrait of Leander's male beauty:

How smooth his breast was, and how white his belly,
And whose immortal fingers did imprint
That heavenly path, with many a curious dint,
That runs along his back.

Those words, along with his poetic depictions of the ways
in which men and even the god Neptune loved Leander for
his beauty, stirred unfamiliar thoughts and feelings within
me, feelings that I did not at that time have the words to
describe, or the ability to fully comprehend.

On another occasion, while lying close together for
warmth on a cold evening in December in our shared bed
at Master Heminges's, Alexander told me the story of one
of the plays he most enjoyed performing in — Shakespeare's
Twelfth Night, or What You Will. He played the role of Viola,
a young girl who during the course of a storm at sea and

subsequent shipwreck is separated from her twin brother, Sebastian, and washed ashore in the land of Illyria. She dresses as a boy in order to survive and so becomes the page to Orsino, a duke who is in love with Olivia and who also seems to have feelings of a sort for his new page, now named Cesario.

It was a role I could easily envision myself playing, but the role I found particularly fascinating was that of Olivia. She falls in love with the "boy" Cesario, and then when the lost twin brother, Sebastian, arrives, dressed in the same clothes and seemingly the same in appearance as Viola / Cesario, she effortlessly transfers her feelings to him, ultimately marrying him.

How, I asked myself, too shy and afraid to ask the question of Alexander, could this be? For Olivia, it appears that the twins are equal and interchangeable. But if this were the case, I reasoned, if falling in love with a woman dressed in the clothing of a man, whose appearance indicated that she was in fact a man, was the same as falling in love with an actual man, what does that mean? Was the only thing that differentiated the two their costume and manner of presenting themselves? Was what Olivia saw and perceived, that there was no difference between the two, the reality?

This was, or so it seems to me, at the heart of the question that has haunted my thoughts and even my dreams throughout my life on stage. What exactly is it that makes one a man? Or a woman? Or is it possible to be composed of elements of both? Is there a difference between how you are seen by the world and how you see yourself?

Thoughts of this, of love and desire, and even, God forgive me, of lust, helped to inform every aspect of my life as an actor, while at the same time being part of the reason why I am leaving this life and beginning another. Often times, the confusion has simply been too much to bear.

Chapter Seven

❧❀❧

In which I go to Hampton
Court and perform for the
royal court

With the commencement of the holiday season in December 1603, the King's Men were honored by being asked to perform before the court of King James at Hampton Court.

We would be presenting *The Fair Maid of Bristow* as well as Master Shakespeare's *Hamlet*, along with his *A Midsummer Night's Dream*. In the first production, I would make my stage debut, albeit in a non-speaking role as a page. I would not appear in *Hamlet* at all, but in *A Midsummer Night's Dream*, I would have my first speaking part, notwithstanding the fact that my role, in its entirety, would consist of a mere five words.

Still, five words in my first play, spoken at Hampton Court before King James and his family and court, was something that six months previous I could not have imagined myself doing. I would play the role of Peaseblossom, one of the fairies asked by the fairy queen, Titania, to attend Bottom, a local workman. Bottom has been innocently caught in the midst of a marital battle between Titania and her husband, Oberon, and Oberon has given him the head of a donkey and has used a magical potion to cause his wife to fall madly in love with him.

My lines, such as they were, were merely the following: "Ready," "Hail, mortal!" "Peaseblossom" and finally again, "Ready." The words were not difficult to memorize, and given that my lines were direct responses to commands from Titania and Bottom, my cues were clear and obvious.

Yet even so, I grew more and more nervous as the evening's performance neared. What if I stammered my words as I had the first time I recited for Shakespeare? What if I did miss my cue? What if I said "Hail, mortal!" when I should be saying "Ready?"

Those thoughts vanished from my mind as we made, as befitted His Majesty's servants the King's Men, the six-hour journey by barge down the River Thames on a cold blustery day direct from the city to Hampton Court. It was the 26th of December 1603, the day of St. Stephen, and we would remain in residence, living in His Majesty's servants' quarters until the 1st of January.

I shall no doubt describe Hampton Court Palace itself at a later time, but for now let it suffice to say that the Christmas festivities held in 1603, the first Christmas of King James's reign, were splendid beyond belief. Every bed in the palace was filled with noblemen and noblewomen from England, Scotland and beyond, as well as ambassadors from Spain, France, Poland, Florence and Savoy, all dressed in their most elaborate robes and finery. There were tents set up surrounding the palace to house the lesser nobility and their entourages. There were continuous balls, receptions, banquets, masquerades, as well as games of tennis and gambling.

All this was to celebrate not only the birth of our Lord Jesus Christ, but to honor our new king along with Her Royal Highness Queen Anne of Denmark, a somewhat bony, sharp-nosed and tight-mouthed woman; their oldest son and heir, Prince Henry, who I believe was nine years old at the time; and his sister, seven-year-old Elizabeth. The youngest child, Charles, had been too sickly to travel, his limbs encased in heavy iron braces since May, when his family arrived in London from Scotland to assume the throne one month after the death of Queen Elizabeth.

Our Royal Highness and Patron, James I, graciously allowed us to perform for the court in the Great Hall. The first evening of our engagement we performed *Hamlet*. Since I did not play a role in that performance, although I would have the good fortune to do so several years later, I was allowed to stand behind the screen at the rear of where we performed, in the pantry area that led back to the serving room. There, I was able to watch the play on the trestle stage, while obtaining a most excellent view of the court and audience in attendance.

The hall, covered from floor to ceiling in elaborate and richly colored tapestries, was brilliantly lit by candlelight, although somewhat overheated due to the large number of people crowded in to watch the performance. (In truth I observed Queen Anne on more than one occasion use her handkerchief to carefully and surreptitiously daub away several drops of perspiration from her forehead.) The entire court hoped to see and be seen by the royal family, although, for the most part, they seemed to spend much of the time talking and whispering to each other throughout the performance, their faces and words hidden behind fans and high-necked ruffs.

For our troupe though, being that it was the first time we had all performed together for a while, and being that it was St. Stephen's Day, and being that we (a word I use loosely since it did not quite, as of yet, apply to myself) were performing before the royal family at Hampton Court, the performance achieved an intensity and power I had hitherto not seen.

Master Burbage was as one possessed playing Prince Hamlet, and Alexander seemed to me particularly piteous in Ophelia's last moments. Every word struck me anew. Each phrase, each speech seemed fraught with meaning I had not grasped when I had seen it previously.

At the end of the performance, because it was their first appearance before the court and in honor of the holiday, Master Burbage, Alexander and the other leading actors were presented to receive the greetings of the royal family. From my hiding place behind the screen, I was able to take notice at the moment when Alexander, still dressed as Ophelia, curtsied, then bowed before His Highness. The king's eyes took on a peculiar gleam, and he smiled in a manner that seemed both intimate and knowing in a way I would not have expected. And while I could not see Alexander's expression in its entirety, a feeling arose within me that when His Highness placed his hand on my friend's shoulder and allowed it to linger there for what seemed an eternity, he was pleased by the king's attentions.

In my naivety and, yes, innocence, I did not yet understand exactly what it meant. And when I asked Alexander about it later while in bed, he seemed to make light of it, telling me that the king had merely told him how much he appreciated his performance as Ophelia.

It was puzzling to me, since Alexander had always been so open and frank with me, but I set it aside for the rest of our time at court. I had other concerns. I had seen the splendor of the court and those in attendance, and worried myself nearly to death that I would somehow fail in my performance, that I would let down all those who trusted in me, that I would be seen as unworthy of my apprenticeship and be sent home in ignominious failure.

I needn't have worried.

We performed *As You Like It* on the 27th of December; *The Fair Maid of Bristow* (a lamentably forgettable play in which I made my debut in a non-speaking role) on the 28th, which was Innocents' Night; on the 30th we performed *The Tragedy of Julius Caesar* before Prince Henry, and then on the 1st of January, again before Prince Henry, we presented (and it seems fitting that here I can at least truthfully say "we") *A Midsummer Night's Dream*.

For me, the performance did go by as if in a dream. Peaseblossom did not appear until the middle of the play, in response to the summons from Titania, beautifully personated by Alexander, then vanished from the scene in the middle of act 4. Thus I spent the first half of the play trembling in fear, then after acquitting myself was able to watch the concluding moments. I listened to Puck's last words to the audience:

If we shadows (*meaning us, the actors*) have offended,
Think but this, and all is mended,
That you have but slumber'd here
While these visions did appear,
And this weak and idle theme,
No more yielding but a dream,
Gentles, do not reprehend:
If you pardon we will mend.

After which, as if to remind the audience that the drama they had just witnessed was indeed but a dream, all of the actors, myself included, returned to the stage to dance a jig to celebrate both the performance itself as well as the audience's and actors' return to the reality of our everyday existence.

For the audience though, that reality still meant a life of relative ease, of luxury and wealth and power. For those of us on stage, the season at Hampton Court had come to an end, and it was time for us to return to a daily life of hard work and performing and the need to reach and appeal to audiences who would purchase tickets for our plays.

And for me it meant the need to continue my apprenticeship, to please my masters, to prove myself as an actor, to begin the transition from small parts to larger roles, and then to play the women's roles I was meant to personate.

Chapter Eight

In which I explain the
workings of the Globe
Theatre, continue learning
how to transform myself into
a woman, and begin to explore
Southwark, the neighborhood
surrounding the Globe

Since the plague was still prevalent in parts of the city, with
three hundred or more dying from the ravages of the disease, the theaters were under orders to remain closed and
were not allowed to reopen until Easter Monday 1604. We
were fortunate in that we were able to live off the money
awarded to us by His Most Gracious Majesty following the
Christmas revels, as well as the additional thirty pounds
that we had been granted from the Chamber Accounts.

During this time, Master Shakespeare returned to his
home in Stratford-upon-Avon, where, I was led to believe,

he would spend the time with his wife and remaining children (his son, Hamnet, having died seven years prior from the plague). He would also compose new plays for the upcoming season, which would commence when the ban on public entertainments was at last ended.

As for the King's Men, we remained outside the city, in Mortlake, for nearly two months. Small groups of actors traveled the surrounding countryside to perform in local towns and villages. Those of us remaining stayed in our lodgings, during which time I continued to work on my gestures and movements, and read as many of the dramas of Masters Shakespeare and Jonson and others as were available. I also buried myself in other works of interest and that added to my education, including *The Book of the Courtier* by the Italian Baldassare Castiglione, which proved to be extremely helpful, not only to myself but to other boy actors of my time.

In this most interesting and singular of texts, the author describes in the minutest of details the manner in which women of quality should both behave and move. Every phrase, every gesture, every movement should be done not in an obvious manner, but simply and as nature would have it.

I had been keeping a ledger of notes for myself of things to learn and remember and use on stage. This from *The Book of the Courtier* struck me as something that I would be able to make good use of when I was finally granted the opportunity to play a woman's role:

Surely, too, you have sometimes noticed when a woman, passing along the street on her way perhaps to church, happens in play or some other reason, to raise just enough of her skirts to reveal her foot and often a little of her leg as well. Does it not strike you as a truly graceful sight if she is seen just at that moment, delightfully feminine, showing velvet ribbons and pretty stockings?

And this also seemed to be at the time a most valuable suggestion, and given the praise I later received — whether earned or unearned I am not altogether certain — I believe it served me well:

I have discovered a universal rule which seems to apply more than any other in all human actions or words: namely, to steer away from affectation at all costs, as if it were a rough and dangerous reef, and (to use perhaps a novel word for it) to practice in all things a certain nonchalance which conceals all artistry and makes whatever one says or does seem uncontrived and effortless.

When the Globe finally reopened in May 1604, it was well over a year since the King's Men had performed there. It had closed on the 19th of March 1603 on order of the Privy Council, when it became clear that Her Highness Queen Elizabeth was near death. While it would have reopened in May, the plague had forced it to remain closed, and so both actors and those who worked backstage were eager for the first productions to begin.

This might be the ideal moment, since the roles I was personating during this period were not necessarily of the greatest interest in themselves, to describe in some detail the others who worked at the theater and relied on it being open to earn their living.

At the front of the house were the gatherers, responsible not only for collecting money from our audience but to then safely store it in a box, in an office specially designed for that purpose. The gatherers were also in charge of the women who sold foodstuffs to the patrons of the Globe, everyone from those fortunate to be well off enough to sit up in the pricier tiers, the heavens, down to those standing in front of the stage, the penny stinkards, whom Hamlet called the groundlings. Beer, hazelnuts, pippins and tobacco were available for sale to all, and, truth be told, much of the theater's income relied on those sales.

In the rear of the theater, there to support the actors, were assistants who played two distinct roles. There was the stage keeper, who served as the Globe's general factotum, repairing what needed to be repaired, cleaning what needed to be cleaned, and doing whatever was required to keep things as neat and orderly as our lead actor, Richard Burbage, demanded.

The book holder's role was far more essential to the actual work done by the actors. When he had been given the original book from the playwright, the book holder would then arrange with the scrivener to produce one full and complete copy written out in his very best hand. This then would be submitted by Master Heminges to the king's Master of the Revels, who would grant his allowance that it might be performed. Although if any of the play's words, phrases or ideas were deemed to be subversive, those items would be struck out, after which the scrivener would copy out again the entire corrected version. He would also make individual copies of each actor's role on long scrolls of paper of remarkably low quality, with their cues clearly and cleanly marked.

Which meant, of course — and this is something that few people outside of the playhouses understand — that no acting member of the King's Men, or that of any other acting troupe, had in their possession a complete version of the text of the play. The cost for providing such was simply too prohibitive. Instead, when the roles for any new play were assigned, the playwright would himself, if possible, be present to talk to us about what he had written, to describe the plot and characters in full, and inform us what he wanted and expected from us as actors.

However, once I became ready to graduate to women's roles, the person backstage on whom I depended the most was the tire man. He was responsible for my wardrobe, and therefore for helping me to present the physical illusion that I was, in fact, a woman.

The custom at that time was to perform on a bare stage with as few indicators of scenery and props as was possible (a custom that, I regret to say, is beginning to change). It was the richly ornate costumes, made from the finest possible damasks, silks, velvets and satins, in an array of colors seldom seen by the vast majority of our audiences, that were the only material tools we had at our disposal to help us bring our illusory dramas to life.

With the houses for public entertainment once again open, Alexander, on one of our rare off days, took it upon himself to take me out to enjoy an example of popular entertainment presented at the theater next door to the Globe, the Paris Garden. It was a favorite of Queen Elizabeth, who though she loved theater would never come herself to the Globe but instead invited the actors to appear before her. The Paris Garden was divided into two separate sections: one featuring bull-baiting and the other, which I would be taken to attend by Alexander, bear-baiting.

I had heard much of this popular entertainment since joining the King's Men, all of whom were in agreement that it was one of the finer spectacles the city had to offer. But after viewing it, I am forced to confess that I was shocked that anyone, after sitting in attendance for more than a moment or two, could find it entertaining in the least.

Standing in a long queue with Alexander, waiting to purchase our tickets, I looked around me, fascinated while at the same time overwhelmed by the swirl of activity. Close enough for us to smell the rotting meat fed to the dogs and the ripe privy smells of their waste were the kennels, from which the howls of what sounded like a hundred beasts could be heard. Nearby, more silent for all that, were the sheds, larger and better built than the kennels, where the bulls and bears were kept.

Closer to the theater I could hear the sounds of music, of dancing and of arguing and fighting coming from nearby taverns. Girls selling sweet treats of all kinds were to be seen, as well as girls selling, as Alexander explained whispering warmly in my ear, their virtue, dressed in long gowns with stiffly starched blue ruffs and tall periwigs towering somewhat precariously atop their heads. They seemed to be in wait for the men departing from the taverns, and, as Alexander described it watching one such transaction, each would settle on a price with her customer before taking him off to what I assumed would be a dark, filthy, flea-ridden abode, or even, if necessary, back behind the dog kennels.

Alexander paid the admittance price that allowed us to sit in the stalls and, taking me by the arm as was his wont, led me in.

My nostrils were immediately filled with the foul stench caused by the vast number of mastiffs, along with that of thirteen large ferocious-looking bears, all locked up in their respective kennels and cages circling the arena. Soon after I entered, my ears were deafened by the roar of the screaming and frenzied and seemingly drunken audience, all eager for the show to begin, all crying out for blood.

One of the bears was a particularly large one who, I was told by a red-faced woman sitting next to me, was the direct descendant of the famous fighting bear named Sackerson. He was so famous, in fact, that Master Shakespeare himself had made mention of him in his popular comedy *The Merry Wives of Windsor*, which we were scheduled to perform in the following week. After the beast was secured to a stake in the center of the arena, several of the great English mastiffs were then set loose.

It was a sight that still brings horror to my mind when I think back on it. The dogs rushed at the bear with much growling and barking and gnashing of teeth. The bear, in return, struck and mauled the dogs, all the while issuing forth such thunderingly angry roars that I found myself tightly clutching Alexander's arm, trembling in fear and trying to contain my nausea. All the while, he and the others in the audience called out for blood, blood and more blood — whether that of the dogs or the bear, I remain not altogether certain.

The dogs threw themselves tirelessly at the bear in the most ferocious manner imaginable, and given the value of the bear to his owners, the dogs often had to be pulled off or their muzzles forced open with long sticks to prevent them doing permanent harm. The teeth of the bear, I was told, were not sharp, but had indeed been broken short so that they could not harm the dogs, although his claws were still sharp and deadly.

As the first group of dogs became exhausted, they were removed from the arena and fresh ones were brought forth to replace them. When the first bear became obviously weary of the fight, another one was brought in to replace him as well, and this continued until all, including the audience, were spent.

Even though the bears were considered too valuable to be killed, the dogs were seen to be expendable and all too easily replaceable. And although I never attended another such entertainment, I shall also never forget the sight, nightmarish as it was, of that first enraged bear, his mouth covered in frothy saliva, his fur red with blood — both his own and that of the dogs he had injured and possibly even killed, either with his claws or, even more grotesquely, by grabbing a dog on the attack and pinching or crushing it to death.

A brief aside — thanks to Master Shakespeare, the memories of that afternoon's questionable entertainment were revived as often as we performed, due to popular demand, *The Merry Wives of Windsor*.

SLENDER
I love the sport well; but I shall as soon quarrel at it
as any man in England. You are afraid, if you see the
bear loose, are you not?

ANNE
Ay, indeed, sir.

SLENDER
That's meat and drink to me, now: I have seen Sackerson loose twenty times, and have taken him by the
chain; but, I warrant you, the women have so cried
and shrieked at it, that it passed: but women, indeed,
cannot abide 'em; they are very ill-favored rough things.

Indeed, they are very ill-favored things, and although I
am not a woman, I am unable to abide them myself.

While the audience left the Paris Garden as happily entertained as though they had attended an event as light and
frivolous as one of the comedies performed next door at the
Globe, I found myself shaken to my very soul. I was hor-
rified not only at what I had seen, but at the blood-hungry
reaction of all in attendance, many of whom it seemed
would not have been satisfied until all available dogs and
bears were lying dead and bleeding on the ground.

Still holding tight to Alexander, I asked him how any
good Christian could take pleasure in such a sight, in seeing God's own creatures tear and kill one another, just for
their foolish pleasure. He looked at me oddly and told me that
he was as good a Christian as one could hope to be. Then he

hugged me and took me out of the theater to a nearby tavern where we drank beer and spoke of other matters until the memory of what I had just seen faded, at least for the moment, from my mind.

Much later that evening, we were rowed across the Thames and walked, or shall I say stumbled, the distance to Master Heminges's home and crawled into bed. I was close enough to Alexander to smell his warm beery breath, and he gave me a quick kiss and began what was to become a new nighttime ritual of rubbing himself against me from behind before falling fast asleep, an action that I at first found perplexing but quickly welcomed as a sign of his friendship and affection, even, I will allow, as the rubbing progressed to something more forceful. Feeling Alexander's body pressing and thrusting against mine, his face burrowed against my neck, I understood, or thought I did, the depth of his feelings for me. As time went on, I not only allowed his advances but encouraged them, often reaching behind me to pull him closer.

But that first night, my thoughts were not of Alexander sleeping beside me but about the events of that afternoon.

I was forced to ask myself the following questions: What was it about me that made me so seemingly different than everybody else? Why did I respond so differently to the bear-baiting? Why did I shrink in horror while everyone else was calling for blood and death? Was something missing in me? Would I always feel like an outsider, like a stranger looking in? And was it this difference that encouraged Alexander's physical advances?

These questions and others I have been puzzling over ever since.

Chapter Nine

In which my training
continues, I am publicly
shamed by Master Ben Jonson
and comforted by Master
William Shakespeare

But of course the time available for so-called forms of rec-reation such as bear-baiting was limited at best. Now that we were able to perform, the theater was open every day with the necessary exception of the Sabbath, and plays old and new, dramas and comedies and history plays, were all acted out on the stage of the Globe. And I was there for all of it.

It would not be an exaggeration to say that the work was, in a word, grueling. And it was work, however much like play it might appear to an audience. That was, indeed, part of our job — to make it look not like work.

It was rare that we would perform the same play two afternoons in a row, which required that the program be changed on an almost daily basis. So if, for example, *The Tragedy of the Spanish Maze* was being performed on Tuesday, rehearsals, such as they were, for Wednesday's play were already taking place, while changes were being made on the play that would be performed on the Thursday. And since the number of players available at any given time was limited due to finances, many actors would be playing two or even three parts in a single production. The demands on one's memory, the need to remember which part one was personating in which play, especially given the fact that nobody involved except the book holder and the playwright himself knew any play in its entirety, was daunting and exhausting both in body and mind.

Even given the extraordinary demand on the other actors, my parts were still, for the most part, as small and unimportant as Peaseblossom in *A Midsummer Night's Dream*. But I was constantly reassured by Alexander as well as Master Heminges that what was important was gaining the experience of being on stage. When roles that suited my abilities were available, I would be awarded them, and in turn the roles would get larger and larger as I proved myself, until I would finally be given the women's roles that I was being trained to perform.

Given the loud and constant demand for new productions from an audience that had not had the opportunity to attend the theater in more than a year, it is perhaps no surprise that the vast majority of those presented at the Globe, and at the other theaters such as the Swan, were entertainments performed one day and forgotten the next. Plays such as the aforementioned *The Spanish Maze*, along with *The Fair Maid of Bristow*, written to instruct men on how to tell a good woman from one that is bad, and *The Malcontent*, *Jeronimo* and *The Tragedy of Gowrie* were all popular but are seldom seen or talked about today.

Two playwrights of that time have stood out though, and their works have been performed often to reflect their popularity with audiences. Their works have also been published in collected editions, making their plays available to those unable to see them on stage or those who wish to read and study them for their further edification.

The first of the two is, of course, Master Shakespeare, whom I have already discussed and who is the playwright whose work has had the largest influence upon me both as a performer and as myself in my own person.

The second of the two is Ben Jonson, with whom I had a much more strained and tumultuous, although ultimately rewarding professional relationship.

He was, to his displeasure, called "the bricklayer" in whispers around the theater although only outside of his presence, since that was the trade, somewhat looked down upon, practiced by his father and his father's father before him.

Jonson though, had received a classical education at Westminster School that, or so he claimed, went far beyond what Shakespeare had received at Stratford. This he never tired of reminding not only Shakespeare but everyone in the King's Men within the sound of his voice, as well as the other theatrical troupes for whom he wrote. For unlike Master Shakespeare, Jonson did not compose exclusively for just one company of actors but went where his services were needed or asked for, or when, because of his temperament, he had to move on to another.

His writing was known and respected for its brilliance. But his reputation for being quick to anger, for having an inordinate fondness for canarie wine, for having no tolerance or patience for fools or criticism or actors not treating his words with the respect he felt they deserved struck a feeling of awe and fright in all who knew and worked with him. (He had in fact been in prison several times, once for killing a man, which he claimed he had been forced to do to defend his own life, although rumors suggested otherwise.)

One morning in the spring of 1604, he arrived to begin preparations for a revival of his comedy *Every Man out of His Humour*, a play that had been performed with great success in 1599 and was itself the second part, as it were, to Jonson's own earlier play, *Every Man in His Humour*. I had read the play in an inexpensive quarto edition I had purchased at the St. Paul's bookstalls, and saw in it a larger, more complex role than those I had up to that time been portraying, one that would test my skills and allow me to prove myself to Masters Heminges and Shakespeare.

The role was that of Fungoso, a law student whose greatest aims in life, it seems, are to have a new stylish suit of clothes and a steady supply of tobacco. And while I was perhaps too young for the role, I plucked up all the courage I had within me and approached Master Jonson to ask him if he might consider me for the part.

Burly and in appearance such that I could understand why they called him the bricklayer, with the oddity of having one eye larger than the other, while the other was positioned lower down his face making it impossible for him to look directly at anyone, he gave the impression of being a man both exhausted from his previous night's entertainments (as I came to understand them to be) and angry with not only the world but with me for having the temerity to speak to him directly.

After looking me up and down twice and informing me that I was too small, too young and, to my astonishment, too boyish and at the same time far too girlish to perform the role as he would like, he still bid the book holder to bring forth the roll. Master Jonson looked through it and pointed out the speech he wanted to hear me read, wherein Fungoso begs his uncle for money for a new suit. And so I began:

> In good faith (*at this point Fungoso looks at the new suit of clothes being worn by Fastidious Brisk*),
> I was never so pleased with a fashion, days of my life. O so I might have by my wish, I'd ask no more of heaven now, but such a suit, such a hat, such a band, such a doublet, such a hose, such a boot, and such a —
> …
> Let me see, the doublet, say fifty shillings the doublet, and between three or four pound the hose; then boots, hat, and band: some ten or eleven pound will do it all, and suit me for the heavens!

I stopped and looked up at Master Jonson, hoping that I had pleased him, but was met with a glare such that would have alarmed and brought a sense of dismay to the most lion-hearted of men. And I, to be frank, was far from the most lion-hearted of men, or, to be more precise, of boys. Jonson shouted at me that I had not yet earned the right to read his words, that I had not even, as he proclaimed in the bluntest and loudest of ways, earned the right to call myself an actor and should, if I had enough of a mind to heed his words of advice, give up any hope of making a success of it and return to my home at the earliest possible moment.

With that, all the hopes and ambitions I had allowed to build up within myself over the past months disappeared in a mere moment. Hoping not to embarrass myself in front of him any further by bursting into tears, I thanked him for his advice. Excusing myself, I ran off to find a hidden area of the theater where I could cry without being seen, and from where, I told myself, I could immediately leave to begin my long shameful walk home to Reading, where I would be forced to confess my failure to my father.

As I sat there in a heap on the floor, weeping on all that would not come to be and wondering how I would be able to explain what had happened to those at home, I looked up to see Master Shakespeare standing over me with a look of concern on his face.

"Never you mind Ben," he told me. "When he sees himself in a looking glass he sees a large bear, roaring at everyone in the world as a truth teller, the only one in the city." And here Shakespeare allowed himself a grin. "But truth be told his only problem this morning was too much wine and carousing last evening.

"But … you do not need to concern yourself about that," he added hastily. "I heard your reading, and while it was not as bad as the angry bear indicated, it was not nearly as good as you can be for two reasons that I know of. The first being that the part of Fungoso is not the sort that you should or will be playing. Fungoso is an ordinary sort of young man, and you, young John, are anything but ordinary. The roles

I know you'll be playing will go beyond ordinary. You have something of magic about you, John, and your roles will have to use what makes you so special.

"But don't let that go to your head. You also read the part badly," and here he laughed softly to himself. "While Ben has many goodly qualities as a writer, writing readable lines for young actors or — and you must promise never to repeat this to anyone, John — parts for any sort of actor is not where his talent lies."

Looking through his seemingly bottomless doublet, Master Shakespeare pulled out another roll — this for young Prince Arthur in *The Life and Death of King John*, which, he told me, we would be performing at the king's court at Christmas, and he would, if I was deemed ready, like me to personate this role.

"I'd like to hear you speak this speech. Arthur is being held prisoner, and his jailer has informed him that he is to be executed in the most horrible way imaginable, by having red-hot iron pokers thrust into his eyes. Imagine yourself then, young John, as Arthur. You're alone, frightened to death and begging him to save your life. You're reminding him of how kind you yourself have been to him while under his protection, hoping against all possible hope that he will take pity on you."

I read over Arthur's words carefully, envisioning myself as that young boy, alone and afraid. I remembered Jonson's words to me earlier, which by sending me home would have condemned me to another kind of death. And so I began:

Have you the heart? When your head did but ache,
I knit my handkercher about your brows,

The best I had, a princess wrought it to me,
And I did never ask it you again;
And with my hand at midnight held your head,
And, like the watchful minutes to the hour,
Still and anon cheer'd up the heavy time,
Saying, "What lack you?" and "Where lies your grief?"
Or "What good love may I perform for you?"
Many a poor man's son would have lien still
And ne'er have spoke a loving word to you;
But you at your sick-service had a prince.
Nay, you think my love was crafty love,
And call it cunning: do, and if you will.
If heaven be pleas'd that you must use me ill,
Why then you must. Will you put out mine eyes?
These eyes that never did nor never shall
So much as frown on you.

I looked at Master Shakespeare with tears in my eyes as
he read Hubert the jailer's next lines in a surprisingly shaky
voice:

I have sworn to do it;
And with hot irons must I burn them out.

A silence filled the corner we were in for several moments
as we considered the impact the scene we had just performed
had had on both of us.

"John," Master Shakespeare said, "I knew my confidence
in you had been well placed. Truth be told, that was as fine a
reading of that scene as I have ever heard. And on your first

reading at that! Well done, John, very well done. The role shall be yours when next we perform it.

"However," he said, "I am not going to let you off without a bit of advice. While reading the lines, consider how and when you take your next breath. The lines and phrases have been kept short for a reason. You are not able, because you are still young and not fully grown as yet, to control your breath as well or maintain a line as long as some of the older actors. That is the reason why, as you shall I hope notice, the speeches I give to my boy actors are, as best as can be done, shorter in length and in the very lines of verse and prose than those I give to the adult actors. Although, as I hope to be able to say, they are equally as strong."

With which Master Shakespeare sighed, rustled my hair, looked deeply into my eyes and said, "So, young John, do not worry about what Ben the Bear said to you. I know who you are and know what you're capable of doing. Indeed … it should not surprise me if you prove to be capable of doing far more than even I imagine. So, young John, my oh so pitiful, oh so young Prince Arthur, I pray you do not let me down."

And with that he took my leave. And I returned to work, vowing that I would never ever let him down.

Chapter Ten

In which I perform before
King James at Whitehall
and before Queen Anne
at the home of the Earl of
Southampton, the roles I am
entrusted with grow larger
and I play my first woman's
part, and Alexander's actions
prove to be somewhat
bewildering

As the period from Christmas to Candlemas approached,
the King's Men were once again summoned by our Royal
Patron King James to perform for himself, his family and
court, as well as his honored guests, both at the Palace of
Whitehall and at one special command performance for
Queen Anne at the home of the Earl of Southampton.

My roles in these plays were as varied as were the plays themselves. Since my reading for Master Ben Jonson had been such a complete and dismal failure, it was thought best by all concerned that I should not perform in the two plays written by him that we performed at Whitehall — *Every Man in His Humour* and the play in which I had so thoroughly embarrassed myself in front of my fellow actors that I refused to even watch the performance, *Every Man out of His Humour*.

One of the plays in which I did play a part, *The Spanish Maze*, was, it shames me to admit, so forgettable that all of us concerned swore to never discuss it again and to forget the name of the play's author as well as the fact that the drama ever even existed. The remaining plays we were commanded to perform for the court were histories, dramas and comedies by Master Shakespeare, whose works appeared to find a receptive audience with His Majesty King James. Because the plays met with his approval, they met with the approval of the entirety of the court as well.

Given my disastrous performance for Jonson, it was decided by Masters Shakespeare and Heminges that comedies, especially those of the more farcical sort, did not match well with my person and whatever talents I might, though still unproven, possess. So I was not given a role in *The Comedy of Errors*, but I was given the opportunity to play the role of Moth in the less farcical, more word-drunk comedy *Love's Labour's Lost*.

In the play, Moth — small and young as I myself was still small and young — serves as page to Don Adriano de Armado, a loud-mouthed braggart convinced of his own elegance and high status, and perfectly incapable of getting to the point of whatever it is he might be trying to say. As Master Shakespeare advised me, Moth's role as Armado's servant is to poke fun at his master.

The speeches I was given were still not of an impossible length for me to memorize — the one that follows was my longest in the play. And thanks to the advice I was given by Master Shakespeare, I was able to read the prose while taking breaths at all the appropriate places in order to keep the flow of words coming as he intended. What I took note of, and I made use of this lesson throughout my time enacting Shakespeare's personages, was that in a speech such as this, he in essence made the prose a list of items of import, making it easier for me both to memorize and to recite:

No, my complete master; but to jig off a tune at the tongue's end, canary to it with your feet, humour it with turning up your eyelids, sigh a note and sing a note, sometime through the throat as if you swallowed love with singing love, sometime through the nose as if you snuffed up love by smelling love, with your hat penthouse-like o'er the shop of your eyes, with your arms crossed on your thin-belly doublet like a rabbit on a spit, or your hands in your pocket like a man after the old painting; and keep not too long in one tune, but a snip and away. These are compliments, these are humours, that betray nice wenches that would be betrayed without these; and make them men of note — do you note me? — that most are affected to these.

This was not the most challenging of roles, but I still took a particular pride in performing it, in particular in the interchanges between myself and Don Armado. The performance seemed to be well received. We performed it three times during the season, including once at the royal request of Queen Anne at the home of the Earl of Southampton, and so I will allow that at the very least my work did not bring shame to the King's Men.

However, what is perhaps of particular interest is that during the course of this season, I finally, more than a year into my apprenticeship, was given my first women's roles — that of the nun Francesca in *Measure for Measure* and a much larger role and what felt like the first test of my ability to become a woman, Princess Katherine in *Henry V*.

The role of Francesca consisted of only nine easily remembered lines, and dressed in a nun's habit that concealed my entire body and a wimple that concealed most of my face as well, it was hardly a worthy test of my ability to become a convincing woman on stage. But for my beloved Alexander, playing the lead role of Isabella was a test he was (I hate to allow, although I must speak the truth) barely able to pass.

He was older now, close to twenty years of age, and his salad days performing women's roles would very soon be behind him. His movements had lost a portion of their grace, and his visage, no matter how well made-up and prepared for the stage, was that of a beautiful young man, no longer that of a beautiful young woman. I, by this time, knew him well enough that I could see the worry and fear lurking behind his eyes. And while it never affected his personation of the novice nun Isabella, it was evident to those who knew him well that he was increasingly aware that his days playing such roles were limited.

This meant, as I had been aware for some time, that I would of necessity soon be taking over the roles that Alexander had excelled in. And that of Katherine of Valois, the Princess of France courted by Henry V in the last act of Shakespeare's play of the same name, would demonstrate to the troupe whether or not my year of training had been effective or fruitless.

Katherine's lines in *Henry V* are minimal, given in short phrases, and, since her command of English was limited at best, spoken in a comic combination of broken English and her native French, which was not outside my abilities. My main test would be that of movement. During the entirety of Henry's wooing of Katherine, the two circle each other in an elaborate dance of courtship, which would show all of the assembled court at Whitehall whether or not I could move, gesture and respond to a man in the manner of a woman of royalty.

I was, I admit, as nervous as I had ever been as I sat behind the stage in the Banqueting Hall. There, after I had worked with the tire man to get into costume — a gown as sumptuous as I'd ever seen with a headtire encircled with pearls atop my head — and had painstakingly prepared my makeup, I caught a glimpse of myself in a piece of reflecting glass. It was the first time I had seen myself not as the boy, John Rice, but as a woman, Princess Katherine of France.

It was a moment I shall never forget — an unsettling experience — yet at the same time one that seemed to inform me of who I really was, in a manner that perhaps I did not need or want to know. Or, that perhaps I did.

When I saw myself, I saw John Rice, the second son of Thomas and Jane Rice of Reading, Berkshire. I also saw the soon-to-be Queen Consort of England, Princess Katherine of France. I was, I thought, both myself and Katherine at one and the same moment. I was also, it seemed to me, both John and Katherine, both boy and girl, in a way I had never before been. A momentary dizziness nearly overcame me as I gazed at my reflection in the looking glass and contemplated who exactly I was or had for the moment become, but then it was time to appear on stage.

It went by all too quickly, as though in a dream. Burbage, who excelled in the role of Henry V, moved with me as though in an intricate dance. Henry's masculinity found a proper balance in my, or should I say Katherine's, reticent femininity that made their wooing and my, or should I say Katherine's, agreeing to marry Henry believable. I sensed that I had the approval of the audience, as well as that of Master Shakespeare and Alexander.

I had passed the test.

For our final performance of the court season at Whitehall, held on Shrove Tuesday, the 10th of February, we performed Shakespeare's comedy *The Merchant of Venice*. Burbage, who had over the course of the previous six weeks so ably personated Henry V, Falstaff in *The Merry Wives of Windsor* and the Duke in *Measure for Measure*, exceeded himself in playing the Jewish moneylender, Shylock. I had the good fortune to personate Shylock's daughter, Jessica, who in the course of the comedy runs away to marry her beloved, the Christian Lorenzo, taking with her a goodly portion of her father's wealth and using, much to the amusement of both the audience and myself, her dead mother's turquoise ring to pay for a pet monkey.

While my part was indeed small — a mere twenty-six lines — it was a pleasure to be on the stage once again with Burbage, for we performed well together. In the same way it was easy for me to be wooed by his Henry V, it was equally easy for me to become his daughter, one who wanted nothing more than to escape a house she described as a very "hell."

It was also a pleasure to watch Alexander portray, for the last time as it turned out, the play's heroine, Portia. In the fourth act, she disguises herself as the male attorney Balthazar to defend the actual merchant of Venice, Antonio, in court from Shylock, to whom he owed a sizeable debt. Antonio ultimately wins a victory and forces Shylock (rightfully, as it seemed to me at the time while immersed in the play) to convert to Christianity.

Alexander was, in a word, magnificent in the role and well knew it himself, as I could sense from the pleasure he took in reciting Portia's big speech, one that garnered special attention and praise whenever the play was performed. When he finished the last line, there was a hush among those in Whitehall's Banqueting Hall, followed by applause that seemed to last an eternity. The play came to a halt, and only after Alexander recited the speech a second time would those assembled allow the comedy to proceed.

When the play ended, while the rest of the King's Men remained on stage, the lead players — Burbage, Alexander and two others — were summoned to be presented to King James. Queen Anne, having seen the play performed at an earlier date, was not in attendance.

His Highness thanked Burbage fulsomely for his portrayal of Shylock, and then, turning to Alexander with a gleam in his eye, he warmly embraced him, one arm lingering on his shoulder before allowing it to slowly drift down Alexander's back until it grazed upon his buttocks before retreating back upwards to complete the embrace. He then summoned a courtier to his side, and, taking a small package from a gold tray, presented it to Alexander, whispering something into his ear.

In truth, I knew not what to make of this considering my close friendship with Alexander. I knew even less what to make of the scene following, when as we removed our costumes to return to our regular manner of dress, Alexander exchanged glances with a young servant girl of seventeen or eighteen who passed among us more times than seemed necessary. He then followed her off, disappearing for a good period of time, before returning to join us as we prepared to depart. I saw the other actors looking at each other and grinning — broad grins that Alexander returned with a knowing nod.

Even so, despite the attention paid to Alexander both by King James and the person I saw at the time as an all-too-forward servant girl, when we left Whitehall to return to our lodgings with Master Heminges, Alexander had his arm around my shoulders. He was laughing as we talked about our success at the court and then whispered in my ear to inform me that despite his general fastidiousness regarding his personage, he had perhaps partaken of too much wine over the course of the evening, which was apparent due to his obvious difficulty in speaking without slurring his words.

But when we finally arrived home, I was the one who was sleeping in his bed, I was the one who was being held tightly in his arms, I was the one who he pressed and thrust his manhood hard against, and who felt warm and safe and secure enough that I felt I could, at least for the moment, banish any thoughts of losing his friendship and his affections to another.

In my hope and optimism, however, and all too soon, I was proven incorrect.

Chapter Eleven

In which Alexander's life
changes, and I find myself
feeling abandoned and alone

Whereas previously it had seemed as if Alexander's time
had been my time, that we had spent both our waking and
sleeping hours together as one inseparable, as winter became
spring, things seemed different. Alexander would go off on
his own, needing, he told me, to explore parts of the city for
which I was not yet ready, to think about what might happen
now that he was outgrowing the women's roles that had made
him well-known among regular attendees at the Globe.

He was also, as I was soon to learn, going off to meet with
the pretty young servant he had had his encounter with at
Whitehall over the holiday season. By May, the girl, Mary
Hastings, was with child, and with the blessing of Master
Heminges, who appeared to be amused by the entire turn
of events, the couple would be joined in holy matrimony as
quickly as was legally possible.

When Alexander, as gently as he could, told me what had transpired and what was going to transpire in the future, I thought, at first, that Mary would soon be arriving to live with us. I could not begin to imagine how all three of us, and then the baby when it arrived, could share the same room, much less the same bed.

I asked Alexander how we could arrange the room to make things comfortable for both Mary and the baby. His initial reaction was to laugh, but when he saw the stricken look on my face, he stopped. Cupping my face in his hands, he told me that he would be remaining with the King's Men, but that given the situation, Master Heminges had released him from his apprenticeship, and that he would begin looking for new lodgings the very next day. He softened the news though, by reminding me that we would still be together every single day, and then asked me if I would do him the honor of being his sole groomsman on the day of his wedding.

I, of course, agreed to do so, despite knowing that with my participation, I was contributing to our parting.

It was warm and the sky was bright on the day of Alexander's nuptials — an omen, I hoped, of good things to come.

Early that morning I accompanied him to a local barbershop where he was groomed and shaved. Alexander was getting shaved two to three times a week in order to keep his skin smooth and feminine, but it would be only a matter of time when no amount of shaving could keep him convincing as a young girl. He and the barber joked about my inability to grow even the slightest hair on my face, even so, I was faintly aware that when that time came, as it must, my days as a boy actor would be nearing their end.

Master Heminges was kind enough to host at a favorite tavern a wedding breakfast consisting of bread of good quality, cheese and beer in unlimited amounts. In attendance were the rest of the King's Men, including even Master Shakespeare himself, to celebrate Alexander's marriage. The bride, who had come to London from the countryside just seven months earlier, was alone except for one or two of the other servants from Whitehall who were able to be in attendance. Even in my sorrow at losing Alexander to her, I felt pity for her lack of family and companionship.

We made a fine sight in our procession to the church. I was honored by Alexander to be asked to lead the way, holding a gilded sprig of rosemary, meant to remind the bride to always remember her holy marriage vows. The King's Men walked behind the nuptial couple, dressed in the clothing issued to them by King James, meant to be worn only at royal ceremonies. Heminges had decided that the occasion demanded that all concerned look their most regal.

The bride, much to my surprise, chose to honor the old tradition, still popular among the residents of some of England's smaller towns and villages but sadly out of date in the city itself. She wore for her wedding nothing but her simplest and oldest smock, a remarkably well-worn undergarment that had seen far better days. By wearing only this in public on the day she was united with Alexander, he would not nor could ever be held responsible for any of her debts.

Throughout the ceremony, I kept my eyes on my beloved Alexander. Seeing the look of happiness on his face, as well as on Mary's, it was difficult for me to begrudge either of them this day. To do so would be purely selfish on my part, placing my friendship above God's wish for us to find happiness and fulfillment in marriage and family.

As we left the church, my feelings of happiness for Alexander along with my own self-centered feelings of pity must have been apparent on my face. Alexander came to me, put his arms around me and held me tight. He assured me that his feelings of friendship and love for me would never change, and bade me vow to never forget that.

We all then retreated to a nearby inn, where Master Shakespeare himself hosted Alexander and Mary's wedding feast. There were heaping platters of beef and mustard, frumenty, mince pies and of course quantities of ale, some of the best of which I had ever had the chance to indulge in.

The festivities continued for the majority of the day, ending only when Master Shakespeare himself, after pounding his tankard on the table to get the attention of all in attendance, stood up, seemingly a bit wobbly on his feet after several hours of imbibing.

"It is an honor for me to be here, to attend and honor the marriage of one of my beloved King's Men, Alexander Cook, to Mary Hastings, whom I just had the pleasure of meeting. And while it might be untoward for me to mention this in public," he said with a slight grin, "it might interest you to know, young Cook, that when I myself got married, some ... well, more than twenty years ago I must confess ... my bride, Anne, was also with child, and all turned out well."

At this point, he chuckled knowingly, about what I do not care to speculate, finished the ale remaining in his tankard, and after wiping his lips upon his sleeve, told the room, "Before we all depart going our separate ways, and before the happy couple go their now-united way, I would like to toast Alexander and Mary." And then, yet again pulling a scrap of paper from his gown, he read:

> Let me not to the marriage of true minds
> admit impediments. Love is not love
> which alters when it alteration finds,
> or bends with the remover to remove.

But then he stopped, mumbling, "No, that is not right …" And then speaking hesitantly as if the words were coming to him for the first time, he said:

> Honour, riches, marriage-blessing,
> Long continuance, and increasing,
> Hourly joys be still upon you!
> Juno sings her blessings upon you.

And sitting down hard on the bench behind him, he called for a pen, appeared to write down what he had just recited and shouted out that with that, our revels had ended. And so they did.

As we variously, dependent on the amount of beer that had been consumed by each, walked, stumbled and teetered our way out of the tavern, the rest of the King's Men silently exchanged looks and nods, at which point they turned to walk down a street that had a look wholly unwholesome. Master Shakespeare turned to me and proclaimed, "And here is where we must part ways, young John Rice. Where we go is not fit for a boy such as yourself, and if I be honest with myself and with you, 'tis not fit for us either."

Heminges and several of the others burst into laughter at the comment. Shakespeare placed a finger to his lips to silence them, and, placing his hand on my head as if in benediction, or perhaps to keep himself from falling over, said, "I leave you now, John, with this."

Assuming a pose I'd seen Burbage take before launching into a speech on stage, he said:

> What early tongue so sweet saluteth me?
> Young son, it argues a distemper'd head
> So soon to bid good morrow to thy bed.
> Care keeps his watch in every old man's eye,
> And where care lodges, sleep will never lie;
> But where unbruised youth with unstuff'd brain
> Doth couch his limbs, there golden sleep doth
>   reign.

"With that, John, we must part ways. And as you know, parting is such sweet sorrow ..." which only served to add to the laughter and general sounds of hilarity from the remaining King's Men, who turned and went down a narrow alleyway, disappearing one by one into the darkness.

I was then left, for the first time since I had arrived in London, to walk back to my lodgings alone. Without Alexander by my side, the way seemed longer and the streets darker and more threatening. The crowds of people, many at this time of the evening, departing loud and red-faced from finishing a night such as the one I had just had at the tavern, had me pulling into myself, withdrawing from the noise and darkness and all that surrounded me.

When I arrived home, I was for the first time sleeping alone, without Alexander next to me, without feeling his warmth, his arms holding me close and keeping me safe and protected from all that caused me to fear, making me feel special and, dare I say, loved.

The bed, which previously had felt small and warm and cozy, had never felt so cold and large.

Chapter Twelve

In which I assume parts of
greater importance, while
those assigned to Alexander
grow less so, and the plague
drives us out of the city

While my outward appearance as I continued working and
training at the Globe remained, as best as I was able to make
it so, one of great cheer, inwardly I remained heartbroken.
I avoided being in Alexander's presence as much as possible, for whenever he was near I found myself unable to
stop looking at him. Feeling my eyes welling up with tears
at what I saw as the loss of my friend, I would turn quickly
away without making it seem as if I was doing so.

This strategy, however, soon proved for naught, because
as our season at the Globe went on, I was given the roles
that Alexander was now too old to play properly, and at the
request of Master Heminges, he was given the task of working with me as I prepared.

The work was hard, as difficult as anything I had yet to attempt. The roles I was asked to personate during the spring and summer of 1605 were of varying types and completely different characters — women of different positions in life, all of whom wanted different things — and I doubted my ability to do them justice.

Indeed, thoughts of failure were ever on my mind; I was frightened that if I should fail, my time with the King's Men would soon be over. Alexander, though, had no doubts, nor did Master Heminges, whose watchful eye was ever present as I rehearsed my movements and learned my lines and cues.

Now is perhaps a good time to note that I was the only actor, both because of my age and lack of experience, who was afforded the luxury of a reasonable, although still not lengthy enough, time to rehearse. For the most part, because time was limited given that we performed almost every day, actors were presented their roles only the morning of the day before the performance. They had at best a few hours in which to memorize their lines and cues or to learn where they would stand on stage along with their entrances and exits, while having to remember all the same for their performance of a completely different play that afternoon.

I was fortunate in that Master Shakespeare, having acted himself upon his arrival in London, seemed to know not only how to write well for actors of all kinds, but how to write for boy actors whose task it was to portray his female characters, in particular. Our roles, although of great complexity and intensity, were, compared to the men's roles, shorter and so easier to memorize. The speeches were, as Master Shakespeare himself had described to me, composed in such a way that the phrases, the breaks in the lines of prose or poetry where I would have to take a breath were on average shorter than those in the men's roles, making them not only easier to recite smoothly, but to memorize as well.

So given that, and given Alexander's help in preparing, the challenge of memorizing my lines and cues, of learning how each character should move, how they would enter and exit, all of the exterior aspects of the character that would easily be seen and applauded or dismissed by the Globe's audience, while a challenge, could, it seemed, be mastered.

What most worried me though was how I, young and inexperienced when it came to life as I was, could begin to comprehend and make believable the lines written for these young girls and women, lines that as I learned them seemed to beautifully express their personages, their dreams and ways of being and thinking and viewing life. These characters, although human, were completely foreign to me, as women as well as in their own beings. Why did they say the things they said and feel the things that they felt? I fully recognized the art in what Shakespeare had put on paper, but how could I read their words in a convincing manner, and by doing so, bring the characters to life, be it Ophelia, Juliet, Viola or Helena?

But as I rehearsed my speeches, read my lines aloud and moved through the scenes, I found myself somehow transforming. I was no longer John Rice, the young boy trying to please Masters Shakespeare and Heminges, as well as my dear friend Alexander, the rest of the King's Men, the audiences and, ultimately and always, God. Instead I was Juliet, desperately in love with Romeo; Ophelia, driven mad because her love, Hamlet, has so cruelly rejected her; Viola, in love with a man in love with someone else; and Helena, in love with a man who says he truly hates her.

Somehow, by some mysterious alchemic miracle, I found it within myself to become each of those women, to become the characters and read their words not as lines in a play written by Master Shakespeare, but as though speaking them for the first time.

If, dear reader, you will allow me to indulge myself albeit briefly, it might be of interest in helping you to better understand the life of an actor that I am now leaving behind by offering examples of what I mean.

While personating Juliet, I became a love-awed thirteen-year-old girl, who while impatiently waiting on her wedding night for Romeo to return, declares that when her beloved dies, the very night itself should cut him into little stars, because the very brightness of his being will then make heaven look all the finer:

> Come, gentle night, come, loving black-browed night,
> Give me my Romeo ...
> Take him and cut him out in little stars,
> And he will make the face of heaven so fine
> That all the world will be in love with night
> And pay no worship to the garish sun.

As I read those lines on stage, I *was* Juliet in love with her Romeo. I was also, in part, John Rice, whose feelings for Alexander had not changed nor ever would.

In the same manner, I became Ophelia, the daughter of Polonius, the councilor of the Danish court, who loves Hamlet. He, at one time, loved her well, but now has cruelly rejected her, a pain that drives her to madness as she, clothing asunder, wanders through the court, speaking to all assembled there:

> There's rosemary, that's for remembrance — pray you love, remember. And there is pansies, that's for thoughts.
> …
> There's fennel for you, and columbines. There's rue for you. And here's some for me. We may call it herb of grace a Sundays. You must wear your rue with a difference. There's a daisy. I would give you some violets, but they withered all when my father died. They say a made a good end.

As I read these lines and moved across the stage, I could feel Ophelia's madness slowly encroaching upon me. Her pain at losing Hamlet and her father was my pain at losing Alexander and my mother. I was at once both Ophelia and myself, and felt close to tears as I presented the rosemary to Hamlet's mother, Queen Gertrude, personated by Alexander, and remembered myself carrying the rosemary at his wedding procession.

And I confess with some amount of embarrassed pride that I espied several teardrops silently rolling down his face at the same time. It was a moment that evidenced that I had done what it was I had meant to do. I had so believably become Ophelia on the stage that even Alexander seemed to believe and accept the illusion and wept for her in her madness as if she was real, and not the same boy he had shared a bed with for better than a year.

If I must write of Helena, and it seems I must, the less I say of her and the play *All's Well That Ends Well* the better. It pains me to speak anything less than the most heartfelt praise for any word that came from Master Shakespeare's pen. But Helena, who loves the oafish dunderhead Bertram with a most unwomanly avidity that strikes one as well nigh unbelievable, who chases after a man who does not love her and who is, indeed, utterly unworthy of her love, was not a role I enjoyed playing, or, truth be told, that audiences enjoyed seeing. I consider myself fortunate that I only personated her three times while with the King's Men.

I can, however, say nothing but the strongest words of praise and love for the delightful Viola and the comedy in which she appears, *Twelfth Night*. It was the first opportunity I had to personate the kind of typical comedic role that Master Shakespeare later told me gave him a great deal of pleasure to write — that of a girl who, like Rosalind in *As You Like It*, is forced by circumstance and fate to spend the majority of the play personating a boy.

"I cannot tell you why it does so," he told me one evening several years later as we sat drinking at the George Inn, "but it tickles my imagination to no end to compose a part for one of my beloved boy actors that allows him to play a girl who then is forced to pretend to be a boy. The audience seems to take a peculiar pleasure in it as does the actor, and for myself, composing the multiple layerings of boys as girls falling in love on stage with other boys, and men falling in love with girls who are really boys amuses me as few other things do."

It amused me as well, since as I have observed earlier, these types of roles were very much similar to the way I felt myself in my relations with others.

Viola, disguised as the boy Cesario, is sent by her master, Orsino, to woo Olivia on his behalf. When Olivia, who has started to fall in love with Cesario, unaware that he is actually a she and has been constant in her refusal of Orsino's love, asks what he would do if he was Orsino to prove his love, I say:

If I did love you in my master's flame,
With such a suffering, such a deadly life,
In your denial I would find no sense,
I would not understand it.

To which Olivia responds, "Why, what would you?"
To which I answer, in my favorite passage of the play:

Make me a willow cabin at your gate
And call upon my soul within the house;
Write loyal cantons of contemned love
And sing them loud even in the dead of night;
Hallow your name to the reverberate hills
And make the babbling gossip of the air
Cry out "Olivia!" O, you should not rest
Between the elements of air and earth
But you should pity me.

To which the only words Olivia can muster are "You might do much."

I understood this speech and Viola all too well, since in a manner of speaking I was John, Cesario and Viola all in one. And need I say that Olivia was personated by Alexander? You could then, if you will, imagine all I was thinking and feeling as I said those lines. It was a bewildering and perplexing experience not knowing which of the three I was, yet at the same time, a moment of great familiarity to me — being someone, or in this circumstance, being some ones, while at the same time still remaining, in some small part, John Rice.

It seemed to be the role that life had assigned to me, and one in which I was, oddly enough, most truly myself.

And in that role, as an actor, my confidence grew with every performance that season. The audiences seemed, indeed, to embrace me and my work. Masters Heminges and Shakespeare told me regularly that I was becoming precisely what they had hoped I would and could be, and at last the King's Men seemed to embrace me as one of their own. I had, after nearly two years of apprenticeship, proved my worth.

There was though one exception to my growing sense of worthiness, and my desire to be absolutely truthful in this telling of my life demands that I must inform you of it. During this time, my dear friend Alexander seemed to distance himself ever so slightly from me, whether because of his marriage and newborn child, because he saw me excelling in roles that had previously been his alone, or because of matters pertaining to our previous closeness that were now painful for him to remember and think on, I do not know. All I do know is that our previous closeness was now fading.

But, truth be told, I was so involved in the performances, in learning my lines and bettering myself that I scarcely had time to look back at what had been lost. New roles followed new roles, and after six days a week of working from light until dark, I was often scarcely able to get myself home before falling into a fast sleep in my bed.

That is until the 5th of October in the year of our Lord 1605, when the theaters were again closed due to the plague ravaging London, and we were forced to flee and find refuge away from the city.

Chapter Thirteen

In which a most audacious
assassination attempt by
the nefarious Guy Fawkes
is thwarted, thereby saving
the lives of the royal family
and all the members of
Parliament, and finally, Master
Shakespeare expresses his
confidence in me

Throughout the month of October, due to the closing of the theaters, the King's Men toured the areas outside London. There, performing where and when we could, we put forth the plays we had recently staged at the Globe, alongside other older plays still popular in the provinces. These included the pastoral romance *Mucedorus*, written by a playwright whose name has since disappeared from the records, and Jonson's *Volpone*, a fine play indeed, but one, as might be assumed, I had no role in. Master Jonson was still the only person not persuaded that I should be allowed to act at the Globe at all, much the less in one of his plays.

And it is perhaps by our own good fortune or the providence of God that we were traveling from Barnstaple to Saffron Walden when word reached us that the Gunpowder Treason Plot, led by the Catholic fiend Guy Fawkes, had been discovered, and the conspirators were quickly being brought to justice.

I have until now avoided writing about the political issues of that time, focusing instead on myself and the theater, but since the plot was so grievous and did impact both my myself and my career in ways most unexpected, I feel it is incumbent on me to give a brief retelling of the events.

The plot, led by the villainous Robert Catesby, a rebel against both his king and his God, was meant to blow up the palace where sat the Parliament for its opening session on the 5th of November, in the hopes that it would bring about a popular uprising. The schemers wanted to bring Princess Elizabeth, James's nine-year-old daughter, to the throne as the new Catholic head of state. The traitorous Guy Fawkes was given charge of the explosives.

But, by the grace of God, the fiendish plot was made known to the authorities in a letter sent to William Parker, fourth Baron Monteagle, and so it was that around midnight of the 4th of November, Fawkes was discovered in the labyrinth of tunnels deep under the Houses of Parliament, guarding thirty-six barrels of gunpowder. This would have been enough to turn the House of Lords to rubble, killing everyone within, including our Sovereign Lord the King; his most excellent and dearest wife, the gracious Queen

Anne; the most noble Prince Henry, their elder son, and so the future hope and joy of England; along with the lords spiritual and temporal, the reverend judges of the realm, the knights, citizens and burgesses of Parliament; and assorted others of the king's faithful subjects and servants, all of whom, with no respect paid to majesty, degree, dignity, sex, age or place, would have been most barbarously destroyed and swallowed up in the explosion.

In truth, had the evil scheme not been prevented, it has been said that more than thirty thousand persons would have perished in a single stroke; the city itself would have been sacked, affecting both rich and poor; and the world would have been witness to a spectacle more horrible and terrifying than any ever before seen. Added to the bodily carnage would have been the loss of all of the repositories of English law and history, along with our greatest architectural landmarks. The Hall of Judgement, the Court of Records, the Collegiate Church, the City of Westminster and even Whitehall itself would have been lost in the explosion and very fires of hell that would certainly have followed.

The king quickly had his justice and revenge. Fawkes was immediately arrested. The remaining plotters largely fled London as soon as they learned their plot had been discovered, and although they tried to find support among the populace along the way, they were largely unsuccessful, and several, including the traitor Catesby, were shot and killed by the pursuing Sheriff of Worcester. Their bodies were later removed from the graves in which they had quickly been buried and then disemboweled. Their various and sundry body parts were sent to the towns and villages from which they came to be displayed publicly. Their heads were sent to London, where they were left to rot on iron poles at Parliament.

I must add here that while upon my arrival in London I had found such a display a shock to my eyes and very system, now I found it fitting judgment. On my daily walk from home to the theater, I watched the heads slowly decay and get pecked at and eaten away by carrion birds.

And of the eight who did survive, including the villain Fawkes, they were put on trial on the 27th of January 1606 and were convicted with great speed and sentenced to be hanged, drawn and quartered.

After the shock of the attempted murder of our king had passed, along with fear and a need to take revenge, a sense of relief and pride in the greatness of our nation swept through the land, as well as a fervent desire to understand where such evil could possibly have arisen from. Heminges seized on the opportunity to not only demonstrate the King's Men's loyalty to our royal patron and our nation, but to also, if truth be told, capitalize on the moment. He put back into our repertory Master Shakespeare's plays historical that tell the stories of Kings Richard II and III, of Henry IV and V and VI, as well as dramas that tell the glorious story of England and the ultimate triumph of Henry VII, the grandfather of our late beloved Queen Elizabeth, and also the great-great-grandfather of His Royal Highness, King James I of England and Ireland.

It would be the 15th of December before the city fathers allowed the theaters in London to reopen, so until then we toured. Audiences came out in large and enthusiastic numbers to thrill to our playing of English history on such a broad and grand scale. Since men are indeed the primary drivers of historical events, the glory of our Virgin Queen Elizabeth notwithstanding, my new roles were somewhat limited — the whore Joan la Pucelle, known by some as Joan of Arc, in *The First Part of Henry the Sixth*, as well as the scheming Margaret of Anjou, who married Henry VI to become Queen of England.

Joan and Margaret were types of personages I had yet to attempt. Joan was a warrior woman, which gave me the opportunity to use my training in those arts. She ends up being rightfully burned at the stake as a strumpet and witch, cursing her captors as she goes:

> May never glorious sun reflex his beams
> Upon the country where you make abode,
> But darkness and the gloomy shade of death
> Environ you, till mischief and despair
> Drive you to break your necks, or hang yourselves.

It was, I must confess, difficult for me to practice those lines without laughing, Joan's anger and way of thinking and speaking being so foreign to my own. But after several attempts, I was able, I think, to play Joan the way that the author of the play intended. Master Heminges was kind enough to not only let me know that he was pleased with the progress I had made, but that he would tell Master Shakespeare as well, for he had gone to Stratford when the theaters closed in order to work on new plays for us.

With the theaters once again open in the city, we returned to London to prepare for the holiday season that was to come. It would be an especially festive celebration, not only of the birth of our Lord Jesus Christ, but also of the miraculous salvation of our king and sovereign and his family from the treacherous plotting of Guy Fawkes and his fellow conspirators.

For the season, we performed for the king and his court the history plays with which we had achieved such success touring England's towns and larger cities. Shakespeare himself was in attendance and seemed to pay especially close attention to my personation of Queen Margaret in *The Third Part of Henry the Sixth*. I was told he watched and listened carefully as I read the she-wolf Margaret's speech in which she taunts the captured Duke of York, causing him to suffer greatly with the news that his son, Rutland, had mere moments prior been unmercifully murdered by her men at her order:

> ... where is your darling, Rutland?
> Look, York, I stained this napkin with the blood
> That valiant Clifford with his rapier's point
> Made issue from the bosom of the boy;
> And if thine eyes can water for his death,
> I give thee this to dry thy cheeks withal.

It is here that I must make my confession. As much as I was learning to take great pleasure in assuming roles that were so far outside of the type I had previously been given and that were, frankly, far outside of the type of personage that I saw myself as being, I was also envious that my Alexander was performing the part of the older Margaret in *The Tragedy of Richard III*, a character who in one moment unleashes her rage against the king:

Stay, dog, for thou shalt hear me.
If heaven have any grievous plague in store
Exceeding those that I can wish upon thee,
O, let them keep it till thy sins be ripe,
And then hurl down their indignation
On thee, the troubler of the world's peace …
Thou elvish-marked, abortive, rooting hog,
Thou that was sealed in thy nativity
The slave of nature and the son of hell;
Thou slander of thy heavy mother's womb,
Thou loathed issue of thy father's loins,
Thou rag of honour, thou detested —

And then later to Queen Elizabeth (not, I assure you, Queen Elizabeth I, but Elizabeth, the widow of King Edward IV, recently murdered by Richard):

Poor painted queen, vain flourish of my fortune,
Why strew'st thou sugar on that bottled spider,
Whose deadly web ensnareth thee about?
Fool, fool, thou whet'st a knife to kill thyself.
The day will come that thou shalt wish for me
To help thee curse this poisonous bunch-backed toad.

Speeches such as these, I was learning, allow the actor the opportunity to perform fully for the crowd, and it is with a strong sense of shame that I admit to feelings of jealousy towards Alexander. I was jealous that the role he was given to enact was one that would so fully draw the attention of the audience, and as well, I must admit, its loud and appreciative admiration of his skills.

As I watched from the rear, listening intently to every word, and again I shamefacedly confess, quietly performing the role, reading the lines and gesticulating to myself, I saw Masters Shakespeare and Heminges watching me, both wearing a look of amusement and curiosity.

Afterwards, Shakespeare, upon whose visage appeared a struggle between bemusement and thoughtful seriousness, pulled me aside to speak, or so he said, on matters of singular importance. Quite naturally, my initial thought was that he was in some way displeased with my work, since I can only assume he was able to read my thoughts on my face, but he immediately dispelled that notion.

"No, young John," he said reassuringly. "You have no need for concern. Burbage and Heminges and I are tremendously satisfied with your work and how far you have come in so relatively short a period of time. You have done my work, our troupe and the king proud." And then, as I breathed an all too audible sigh of relief, and as the tension in my body eased, he asked, "Do you think you are ready for your first lead part? Your master and myself are both convinced that you are, but tell me, John, and there is no shame in telling me otherwise if you don't think yourself ready. But let me tell you as sure as I am standing here, I believe you are. So what say you?"

I was unable to speak after hearing Shakespeare's words of confidence in me, but once again it seemed that my face, which undoubtedly expressed my astonishment and pleasure, told the story.

"Fine. The play is not yet complete, but I can tell you this — it will have witches and murder and demonstrate what befalls those whose ambition leads them to murder. It will be dark and gloomy, and will at the same time demonstrate that it is fit and right and just that James I should be our king.

Your role, John, that of Lady Macbeth, will be by far the most complex and, in some ways, villainous one you have ever had the opportunity to personate. She will begin as a loving wife who, pushing her husband on to what they both see as greatness, encourages him to commit murder — not just murder, mind you, John, but murder of the king in their own home while he is under their protection. Her ambition for her husband will ultimately end in their mutual destruction. Macbeth, who becomes a ruler most tyrannical, will be killed by an army that wishes to put the rightful leader on the throne, and Lady Macbeth, who will be driven mad by her crimes, and … to be honest with you, John, I am not certain yet how she will end. I am still working that out in my mind. Perhaps you might be able to suggest something for me?"

At this point he laughed, as did I.

"What concerns me, John, now that all involved in the nefarious Gunpowder Plot have been given the justice they deserved, is how and why it could have happened. Not merely the specific political and religious reasons for the plot, but in a larger sense how does a seemingly normal if ambitious Scottish nobleman become a murderous tyrant and perform such truly unthinkable and unutterable acts of violence? What sorts of lies and stories and pretended reasons do such men tell themselves to justify their actions? Is the source of their evil within themselves, or are they being acted upon by outside forces?"

At this point Shakespeare, who had seemingly become carried away with his own thoughts, glanced at me with a slightly embarrassed look on his face and so continued.

"At any rate, my young friend, with your help I am certain that we can make the play a success and one that will, I fervently believe, establish your reputation throughout London as an actor with gifts most special. May I rely on you, John, to work hard and to trust in me that I will do everything in my power to help you and be there for you every step of your path?"

As he said those words, I could feel my heart swell with pride and determination. I felt stirrings within me of a greater ambition than I had known as of yet. Not only would my playing of Lady Macbeth demonstrate to Master Shakespeare as well as Master Heminges and the rest of the King's Men that their trust in me was not unwarranted. It would, if all went well and according to God's will, show the world what I, John Rice, was capable of. That in my personal singularity I was perhaps capable of greatness.

Chapter Fourteen

In which I work closely with
Master Shakespeare while
preparing to personate Lady
Macbeth

It was during the midst of our regular season, in March 1606, that Shakespeare came to me to let me know that his play, now formally titled *The Tragedy of Macbeth*, was for the most part complete. He requested that I come to his lodgings the following morning so that we could work in quiet seclusion without the hurly-burly and constant distractions found every day at the Globe.

I was honored and flattered not only that he would be taking the time to help me do his work all good justice, but that he would ask me to enter his home. It was well known among the King's Men that while at the theater Master Shakespeare was most approachable, when he left the Globe, his life and home were his own. So I went dressed in my finest attire, which had been given to me at the beginning of the year by Master Heminges as part of my apprenticeship, instead of appearing before Master Shakespeare in the usual mix of clothing passed on to me by Mistress Heminges as her own children outgrew it.

Even so, despite being fittingly dressed for the occasion, it was with feelings of nervousness that I walked from the Heminges's family home to the corner of Silver and Muggle streets in Cripplegate where Master Shakespeare took lodgings with Christopher and Marie Mountgay, makers of fashionable headwear for ladies of the court. I knew not what to expect when I knocked at his door and heard him shout, "Come in, John. You're punctual as usual."

I was pleased to see a home like that of any other man — simple furniture, what seemed a bed of good quality, all kept as orderly as one could expect, with the exception of the writer's work area. There were to be seen parchments strewn about, pens of various and sundry stages of usage, inkpots as well, and as might be expected, volumes of books piled around the edges of the desk. Seeing my interest, Shakespeare allowed me to look closely at the ones he described as his "most treasured companions."

There was a fine set of *Holinshed's Chronicles of England, Scotland and Ireland*, which he told me he had made fine use of during the writing of *Macbeth*. There were several volumes of Plutarch's *Parallel Lives*, and while telling me "there are fine stories to be found in them," his face wore a look of surprised and pleased inspiration. There were copies, both in Latin and in English, of what seemed to be much-loved and much-pored-over editions of Ovid's *Metamorphoses*, "which, young John, I suspect you know well from your schooling." There was a work new to me, *Essays* by Michel de Montaigne, and the most well-worn volume of the lot, John Baret's *Alvearie,* which was, as its full title makes clear, *An Alvearie or Quadruple Dictionary, containing four sundry tongues, namely, English, Latin, Greek, and French, newly enriched with a variety of words, phrases, proverbs, and diverse lightsome observations of Grammar* — a source of great information that I had used during my school days, and one that it seemed Shakespeare consulted on a daily basis.

And so after clearing away space around his writing table for us both to sit, as well as gently pushing away a large orange-colored cat ("move away, Tybalt," he affectionately told him, "we must work"), Master Shakespeare presented me with a parchment manuscript. Written in his own hand, it included not just my lines with the cues as was customary when presented one's roll at the Globe, but all the scenes in which I, or should I say Lady Macbeth, appeared in their entirety. This was a luxury that allowed me not only to know my own lines, but those of the other actors in those scenes, which I much appreciated. It was an opportunity to get a sense of not only what the play would be about, but the role that Lady Macbeth played in the story.

We read through my scenes together. Shakespeare started off by laughingly informing me, "It's been quite a while since I have acted, and as anyone who has ever seen my work on the stage will swear to, John, I am, as I say with all due modesty, a far better writer of plays than I ever was an actor of them."

Regardless of his protests though, as we read through the first half of the play, the portion in which the majority of my acting took place, I could, as we progressed, witness a change in the way he read his lines, so that what began as a slow and deliberate reading became, steadily and surely, a performance. Indeed, Master Shakespeare changed before my eyes into Macbeth.

When the play begins, Macbeth is Scotland's Thane of Glamis under King Duncan, but as he fulfills the prophecy of the three Weird Sisters, who were in truth the witches that Shakespeare promised me, he becomes Thane of Cawdor, and then, pushed on by his wife to murder Duncan, King of Scotland.

As I read my lines for the first time, I placed my concentration on getting a sense, an initial knowing, of who this lady might be. And I confess, as I said the words aloud, I shuddered at her evil ambition. Yet at the same time I was pleased, knowing that if the words and lines were said as they were meant, that if I could transform myself into this seeming monster (as at least she appeared to me in the first half), that the impact I could make on an audience would be a considerable one, surpassing even, I imagined if just for a moment, anything Alexander had accomplished in his career.

Master Shakespeare, who seemed to be able with just a glance to discern my thoughts and emotions, cautioned me as we stopped work for the morning (he having other things to attend to and myself needing to hurry over to the Globe for the afternoon's performance) to take care with one particular aspect of my playing the lady.

"It will be too easy, John, I think, to present the lady as pure evil. I would hope that you will be able to avoid that. Do not play her as a villain in one of Kit Marlowe's dramas," here he chuckled and gave me a look to see if I fully understood what he was saying, "or in Kyd's *Spanish Trag-edy*. Or even as you saw Burbage performing Richard III at Whitehall after the New Year. Burbage is as great an actor as I've seen and his Richard is everything I would want it to be, but Richard is a very different kind of character than that of Lady Macbeth. Richard exalts in his evil, he enjoys being evil and plotting, and even more to the point of what I am saying is that he shares his enjoyment of being evil with the audience. That is exactly what I do not want for the lady.

"Instead, John, what I want to see you do is this — personate her, play the role of Lady Macbeth, but not as someone who wallows and exalts in their own villainy. Play her instead with more subtlety, as someone who does not know that she is a villain. Play her as someone who convinces herself that what she is doing is good and right, but whose discovery by the end of the play that she is indeed a villain, and is indeed evil, is what drives her mad. Can you do that for me, John?"

I returned the next morning, when Shakespeare and I read through the last portion of the play and my last scene in which Lady Macbeth's madness is made clear. Then we went back to the beginning, where with painstaking exactness I was slowly led through each of my major speeches.

"It is not a role of great length," he told me as a way of reassuring me. "Poor Burbage has more than seven hundred lines to learn," and here he gave me a wink, "which at his age will be no small challenge. You, John, have 259 lines, nothing for a boy with your prodigious skills at memorization. But I promise you this, each and every line counts for much. And as I have written Lady Macbeth to be played by you and only you, young John, I have attempted, despite the complexity of some of the speeches (and indeed, they are the most complex you have yet encountered) to make the phrasing well within your abilities."

"So, John, let us begin again with the lady's first speech, reading a letter she has been sent by her husband, Macbeth, telling her of the predictions of the Weird Sisters.

> They met me in the day of success, and I have learned by the perfectest report, they have more in them than mortal knowledge. When I burned in desire to question them further, they made themselves air, into which they vanished. Whiles I stood rapt in the wonder of it came missives from the King, who all-hailed me "Thane of Cawdor," by which title before these weird sisters saluted me, and referred me to the coming on of time, with "Hail King that shalt be." This have I thought good to deliver thee, my dearest partner of greatness, that thou mightst not lose the dues of rejoicing by being ignorant of what greatness is promised thee. Lay it to thy heart, and farewell.

"Note this, John. The letter is prose, which you should be able to read as it is like to your everyday speech. The lady is seen here for the first time reading aloud the final part of the message from her husband, since it is apparent he has already told her about his victory in battle, and apparently as well, about the Weird Sisters, the witches I promised you. Do you believe in witches, young John? I confess, I do not, but our King James does, quite strongly in fact. Indeed, he has even written a book on the topic, which is one of many reasons I have included them in this play. This speech should be quite easy for you to understand and impart to the audience, correct?"

Here I nodded, although I had my doubts but did not want to disappoint Master Shakespeare by saying otherwise.

"And so then, let us move on.

Glamis thou art, and Cawdor; and shalt be
What thou art promised. Yet do I fear thy nature,
it is too full o' th' milk of human kindness,
To catch the nearest way.

"This too should be fairly easy for you to speak, as well as to understand. When she says about her husband 'Yet do I fear thy nature, / it is too full o' th' milk of human kindness / To catch the nearest way,' what is it that she is concerned about?"

I hesitantly answered that I believed that she was wary of his willingness to do whatever it might require to take the next step to become king, and to do so in the fastest way; that he was, "too full o' th' milk of human kindness / To catch the nearest way," meaning by this the fastest way to become king. And while I was uncertain that I was correct and that I was able to please him with my response, it was apparent that I did.

"That is a good place to begin your way of considering Lady Macbeth. Now, I'd like you to think carefully on these things as you learn this role and the last lines of this speech. Earlier in the play, Macbeth himself has suggested that he has previously considered the need to kill Duncan in order to advance his ambitions. And now Lady Macbeth has suggested the same thing. Have they discussed the possibility together? Have they arrived at the same conclusion separately? That is something for you to think about as you think about the character, and think as well on the last lines of her speech:

Hie thee hither,
That I may pour my spirits in thine ear,
And chastise with the valour of my tongue
All that impedes thee from the golden round,
Which fate and metaphysical aid doth seem
To have thee crowned withal.

"Imagine, John, the lady's poisonous tongue in her husband's ear, pouring forth her venomous thoughts and ambitions, pushing him on to commit an act of murder that he himself is hesitant to perform. Consider all that this tells you about her nature and her willingness to be as ruthless as necessary to push him to overcome that which keeps him from seizing the crown, what she calls — and I must shamefacedly admit that I am rather proud of this image — the 'golden round.'" At which point, to my utter bemusement, he gave me a grin brimming with pride at what he had written.

I was, I admit, starting to feel overwhelmed. Master Shakespeare was in such a state of excitement that his explanation was beginning to be lost on me. But as he continued, I did my best to follow along and hoped that when I read the play again myself at a later time, it would begin to make sense.

"Now, on to the third speech, given, as you know, when the lady has received word from her husband informing

her that King Duncan will be arriving that night, presenting her and Macbeth, who will arrive home shortly before
their guest, the perfect opportunity to … 'catch the nearest
way.' Some of the language is, I know, complicated, and her
thoughts are circling around what can only be thought of
as a dark place as she envisions creating her own hell in her
castle:

> The raven himself is hoarse
> That croaks the fatal entrance of Duncan
> Under my battlements. Come, you Spirits
> That tend on mortal thoughts, unsex me here,
> And fill me from the crown to the toe, top-full
> Of direst cruelty! make thick my blood,
> Stop up th' access and passage to remorse;
> That no compunctious visitings of Nature
> Shake my fell purpose, nor keep peace between
> Th' effect and it! Come to my woman's breasts,
> And take my milk for gall, you murdering ministers,
> Wherever in your sightless substances
> You wait on Nature's mischief! Come, thick Night,
> And pall thee in the dunnest smoke of Hell,
> That my keen knife see not the wound it makes,
> Nor Heaven peep through the blanket of the dark,
> To cry "Hold, hold!"

"Think about it, if you will, like this, with the poetry and
pretty language removed, with just its essence remaining:

"Even the raven, the black, evil harbinger of death that
croaks the news of Duncan's fatal entrance is hoarse, she
says out loud. She — meaning you — closes her eyes and

raises her arms up to the sky, calling on the spirits that tend on mortal thoughts to take away all that makes her feminine, meaning gentle and womanly, and instead to fill her completely full of the most dire cruelty. She calls on the spirits to make her blood thick to prevent her from feeling the slightest bit of pity, so that no natural feelings of goodness or humanity can get in the way of her evil scheming.

"She then puts her hands on her breasts, summoning those same spirits to remove their nourishing milk and fill them instead with gall most bitter and poisonous. Keep in mind the very fact that she is summoning spirits to provide assistance; consider whether that provides a link, a commonality between her and the witches. She calls on the thick darkness of night to shroud and keep her hidden with the dunnest or murkiest smoke of hell, a smoke so dark that the knife she uses will not be able to peer through it to see the wound it makes, so dark and murky that not even the light of heaven will be able to peer through it to cry out for her to stop! Stop!"

When he paused to catch his breath, I took a deep breath myself, wondering whether I'd be able to portray such a monster in a way any close to believable. But then I recalled to myself Shakespeare's words of the previous day, not just his words of trust in me, but his words advising me to think of her as someone who does not know or think of herself as evil.

Thinking of her in that manner, it seemed to me, made her actions more understandable. She was doing whatever she thought was necessary to achieve her goal for herself and her husband, and nothing else mattered, even, I slowly understood, the ideas of good and evil. It was something, as

I thought about my own rapidly growing ambition to make my mark on the stage, that I could understand and even, if I pondered it deeply and honestly, feared taking place within me.

"Before you go off to the Globe and I go off to …" here he smiled again, "go off to whatever it is I must go off to, consider these things. In the speech we just discussed, take note of how I play with the sounds of words as I did with Arthur in *King John*. Hear how the hard sound of the letter 'c' bounces off with the softer sound of the murmuring 'm' which, if I can trust my own ear, will help to convey to the audience the sinister nature of her speech and of the lady herself.

"As well, think on this. Think about the darkness that permeates every moment of the play, from the darkness that the Weird Sisters introduce in the very first moments of the drama to the shadows and fog that envelop every moment thereafter. Think about the blood saturating the play, from King Duncan's first lines referencing a "bloody man" to the battle scenes and beyond. By my own count I used the word more than forty times throughout the play. Macbeth envisions daggers covered with blood before his eyes. The lady is unable to clean Duncan's blood from her hands during the sleepwalking scene, which we will go over soon." And then, giving me a curious smile, he added, "This will be the moment in the play, John, that will prove your worth for all to see. Even brave Macbeth, after butchering his guest and king, finds himself covered, literally and metaphorically, in blood.

"These aren't your lines, John, but bear them in mind while you think about the play.

Will all great Neptune's ocean wash this blood
Clean from my hand? No, this my hand will rather
The multitudinous seas incarnadine,
Making the green, one red.

"Imagine that, John, being so covered in blood that not
even the ocean itself can wash you clean. Macbeth has that
sense from the moment of the murder. It will take your
character, the lady, longer to see that she, too, is covered
in blood, blood that cannot ever be removed from her soul
and conscience."

I shuddered here for a moment, seeing in front of me not
only Lady Macbeth covered in blood, but the blood-covered
beasts at the bear-baiting I had seen with Alexander. Were
we really so far above them as I had thought?

"And not just the blood. Recall, John, when we first
spoke of this play, when I told you that one of my reasons
for writing it was to try to determine, or at least to present
the question for the audience to consider, is the source of
evil, in this case that of Macbeth and his lady, is it created
by demonic forces outside themselves? Or is it something
that is found within them? Is the living hell that they will
experience and, indeed, unleash upon all of Scotland, created by the witches seen by Macbeth and the spirits called
upon by Lady Macbeth, or is it their creation alone? And on
that most cheerful of notes, we must part."

And so we went through the play together each morning, talking about each scene, the lady's lines and why she
was saying what she was saying, where I should breathe and

which words should be given emphasis, and what I should think about while reading and becoming the lady.

When we arrived at Macbeth's doubts about the rightness of murdering the sleeping king, and when I read the lady's lines, the lines I myself would be speaking, boasting of her capacity for cruelty, I shuddered:

I have given suck, and know
How tender 'tis to love the babe that milks me:
I would, while it was smiling in my face,
Have plucked my nipple from his boneless gums,
And dashed the brains out, had I so sworn
As you have done to this.

I was unable and unwilling to believe that any woman would say such things about an innocent infant babe. But as I was becoming aware, as the play was teaching me, we as humans, especially when we lose God as the lady did when she summoned the evil spirits to her, are capable of any amount of cruelty.

But then as events unfold on the night of the murder, she proves incapable of performing the act herself, because as she tells her husband after laying out the daggers near Duncan's sleeping body:

Had he not resembled
My father as he slept, I had done't.

Was this a seeming last gasp of her humanity, of her conscience holding on against the evil surrounding her? I was not altogether certain, but I knew it was something I would be able to hold tight to while playing her, to remind me that despite everything she still has some vestiges of conscience remaining.

We made our way painstakingly through the play as the horrors piled upon each other, as Macbeth ordered the murders of Banquo, of Lady Macduff, of one innocent after another, as fear and ambition drove him to such cruelty that even nature, after the unnatural murder of the king, began to rebel against itself. Owls killed hawks, and, most horribly, as man turned against man, horses turned against horses and began to devour each other.

By play's end, the nightmare that was life in Scotland and Macbeth's castle comes to an end. Macbeth is killed in battle, and Malcolm takes his rightful place on the throne. But before that event occurs, the lady has her final scene, one that in its own way is just as chilling as any before.

The lady's gentlewoman-in-waiting is found talking to a doctor about her mistress's nightly sleepwalking. She describes how the lady has a candle with her at all times to dispel the darkness while, most piteously, constantly rubbing her hands together as if to wash them clean.

As they comment, Lady Macbeth, unseeing, approaches and speaks:

Out, damned spot: out, I say. One; two. Why then 'tis time to do't. Hell is murky. Fie, my lord, fie, a soldier and afeared? What need we fear? Who knows it when none can call our power to account? Yet who would have thought the old man to have had so much blood in him? …

What, will these hands ne'er be clean?

...

Here's the smell of the blood still: all the perfumes of
Arabia will not sweeten this little hand. Oh! Oh! Oh!

Despite the evil nature the lady has shown throughout
the preceding drama, it was difficult to read these lines,
much less speak them aloud without feeling some sense of
pity for the suffering woman, driven mad by her role in the
murders and her inability to wipe the blood and guilt off
her hands.

These are Lady Macbeth's last lines in the play. She never
again appears upon the stage. Moments later, the audience,
along with her husband, learns that the lady has died a most
unnatural death. Whether she has fallen or thrown her own
life away by leaping to her death is never made clear. To this
day I still wonder if, as Master Shakespeare indicated when
he spoke to me about the play that very first time, he himself was unsure of how it is that she dies.

I knew though that how I played this scene would be of
the greatest import. If I was not able, through my movements and reading of those few lines, to bring the audience
to pity and even tears for this most horrible of women, what
Shakespeare was trying to show would be lost. The lady
would prove to be a mere villain instead of a woman, seemingly no longer unsexed, who in a curious but real way ends
up as a victim of her own acts of evil.

I was, I must confess, desperate to prove not only to
myself but to Shakespeare, Heminges and the rest of the
troupe that I could portray more than innocent young girls
or small yet dramatic roles such as Queen Margaret. I could

fully personate a complete character — one who has not just a single aspect to her being, but many. I could portray a woman who begins the play as one thing, but who, over the course of the drama, changes, not only because of the events that unfold throughout the play but who changes in her own person as well. And I must allow, although it perhaps sounds like a boastful display of pride in my own talents, I had the growing confidence that I would be able to do it, to bring Shakespeare's creation fully to life.

Chapter Fifteen

In which rumors sweep
London, we perform *Macbeth*
at the Globe, and another new
drama by Master Shakespeare
both puzzles and dismays
audiences

Working with Master Shakespeare in private had been a great assistance in my preparations for personating Lady Macbeth, assistance for which I would remain forever grateful. But it was a very different matter when the time came to rehearse with Burbage, who would, of course, be playing my husband, Macbeth, along with the rest of the King's Men, including Alexander, who was given the prime role of Macduff.

Performing and even rehearsing with Burbage was, each time, an intensely intimidating experience for me, regardless of how often we worked together. Burbage was renowned as the finest tragedian of our time, having played and made his name, along with those of the plays, personating Richard III, Othello and Hamlet. Each role differed completely from the other, yet each was so fully inhabited and personated by Burbage that it was difficult to believe that the same actor played them.

It was known by all that Burbage so transformed himself into whichever character he was asked to portray, that from the moment he was costumed until the moment the play was complete, he was never himself, only his character. And it was said, too, that audiences were never more delighted than when he was speaking on stage, or more sorry than when he was silent. Yet even then, through the power of his movements and very presence, they were still fully in his thrall.

It was then regardless of the fact that I had been paired with Burbage on more than one occasion, albeit in smaller roles for myself, and regardless of the fact that I had been acquainted with him for almost two years, that I remained in awe of his talent. I was intimidated by the masculine force that emanated from his very soul, and unsure if I, now fifteen years of age, could perform the role of his wife. Could I not only stand up to him as an actor, but also portray the kind of power that the lady had over Macbeth, a power that would help convince him to ignore his conscience and murder the king?

I need not have worried. Burbage, sensing my unease at taking control from him, made it easier than I would have imagined. And since he, from the first moment of our first rehearsal became the Macbeth that was Shakespeare's creation, I was able to become the Lady Macbeth that was Shakespeare's creation just as smoothly. Although, I admit, it would not have been possible without my earlier tutoring from the playwright himself.

To my surprise, it was a mere matter of reading Shakespeare's lines as he meant them to be read and making the leap of imagination necessary to perform an internal form of negation to think of myself not as John Rice, nor to think of the actor opposite me as Richard Burbage, more than twenty years my elder, but to think of myself as Lady Macbeth, ambitious for her husband and herself, and willing to do whatever was necessary to push him forward.

It was a startling feeling of power during our first rehearsal to express the lady's outraged scorn, her questioning of his very masculinity, and to then see and hear Burbage respond fully, not as the actor I had become friends with over the last years, but as Macbeth. When hesitating to go forward with their plans, he tells her of his fears, and with my own eyes I saw Burbage, or in actuality, Macbeth, blanch and tremble in response to my words of scorn. At that moment, I could feel not only the lady's power, but my own power as an actor. It was a moment I have never since forgotten.

It was in the midst of our preparations on the 22nd of March, with tensions still high after the revelation of the Gunpowder Plot, that rumors swept through the city that King James I had been assassinated. The uproar was instantaneous and amazing, as fear of mob violence reached every corner of London. Soldiers were placed in every ward and armed guards at each of the city's gates. Fortunately for all, the rumors were false. The king was very much alive, and upon hearing the news of his demise, he presented himself to the public at Knightsbridge, where his subjects, I among them, fell to our knees, speechless with tears of joy.

The sounds of bells and fireworks were heard throughout the city, and Jonson, whose seeming contempt for me had not diminished in the least despite or perhaps because of Shakespeare's patronage, took it upon himself to ingratiate himself with our king. He wrote a poem, "To King James, Upon the happy false rumor of his death, the two and twentieth day of March, 1606," that was such an obvious attempt at currying favor that it diminished him greatly in the eyes of all who knew him, something from which, I must confess, I took an unhealthy satisfaction.

The day the poem appeared for sale at one of the bookstalls at St. Paul's, Heminges sent me out to purchase a copy. When I returned, quickly as he requested, he read it to himself, started laughing, then presented it to Master Shakespeare, who was standing close by. Shakespeare read it, burst out laughing and then called upon us all to attend him while he read it aloud:

> That we thy loss might know, and thou our love,
> Great heaven did well to give ill fame free wing,
> Which, though it did but panic terror prove,
> And far beneath least pause of such a king;
> Yet give thy jealous subjects leave to doubt,
> Who this thy 'scape from rumour gratulate,
> No less than if from peril; and devout,
> Do beg thy care unto thy after-state.
> For we, that have our eyes still in our ears,
> Look not upon thy dangers, but our fears.

At which point Master Shakespeare gazed at us all solemnly for but a moment, then allowed a gigantic smile to slowly make its appearance before he exploded in helpless, raucous laughter.

"Heminges," he said, "Jonson calls himself a poet? With this?" He shook his head. "'Look here, Your Highness. Nobody loves you as much as your good servant Ben Jonson' is what he is saying by rushing this so-called poem into print. Of all the obsequious ..."

Shakespeare's rant against Jonson's poem and attempt to curry favor with the court of King James went on for what seemed like minutes, as his multitudinous talent with words and language poured forth in amused contempt towards his fellow poet.

But when he had finished, it was time for us all to return to work, for our first performance of *Macbeth* was just two days away.

As I stood behind the stage in the tiring-house with the rest of the King's Men, I heard the single blast of a trumpet signaling that the performance would shortly commence. Then a second blast as the crowd came in. And then the third, triumphantly announcing that we were about to begin. I ran my hands over my gown, the corset tightly wrapped to shape me into a woman's form, and examined myself closely in a small looking glass to ensure that the white makeup completely covered my skin, making my eyes look even larger and more expressive than normal, or so I hoped.

I heard my cue, Banquo's lines:

Whose care is gone before to bid us welcome:
It is a peerless kinsman.

I waited for him to exit the stage and made my entrance, gliding out in my most womanly manner, clutching the letter from my husband, Macbeth. I was now no longer, in my own mind and heart, John Rice. I was Lady Macbeth, learning of my husband's encounter with the witches. I began reading softly at first, and then with steadily increasing excitement and passion.

"They met me in the day of success: and I have learned by the perfect'st report ..."

The rest of the performance disappeared into mystery for me. John Rice was not himself on the stage. Instead John Rice was personating Lady Macbeth, saying her words, feeling what she felt, raging and pushing at her husband — at *my* husband — to be great, cleaning blood from the daggers used in the murders, and finally, overcome by guilt at what I had done, falling into madness and death.

I do remember the hush that fell over the crowd during that first performance as the news of the murder of King Duncan was announced. I remember Burbage's hands — my husband, Macbeth's, hands — on me, and his pain and rage. I remember how during the sleepwalking scene my hand shook as I held the candle, as the lady's emotions became mine, or perhaps mine became hers. I remember the roar of the crowd at play's end, when Macduff, who had bested my husband in battle and ended his evil reign, entered carrying Macbeth's head in his hand.

I remember the moment of silence at Macduff's final words announcing the death of Macbeth and the naming of the new king, and then when we all returned to the stage, I remember the roar of applause. I saw Shakespeare smiling proudly at us, perhaps at me in particular, while also taking in the reaction of an audience whose pleasure at his play pleased him as well.

And finally, I remember dancing the jig with Burbage, signaling to the audience that the performance was over, then walking back to the tiring-room where he shook my hand, then hugged me and kissed me on the cheek, as though uncertain who it was he was acknowledging, and telling me that for those hours on stage I had been Lady Macbeth.

I could not have been, God forgive me, more proud of myself and what I had done.

Shakespeare was not, however, the only playwright whose plays we staged at the Globe. Over the next several months, we performed plays of varying quality, including two more performances of *Macbeth*, yet another revival of *All's Well That Ends Well*, dramas such as *The Miseries of Enforced Marriage*, along with others performed once or twice and then forgotten.

There was, though, another new play of Master Shakespeare's, *The Tragedy of King Lear*, which we presented for the first time in late spring of 1606, and it did not receive the same reception as *Macbeth*.

I know not what inspired Master Shakespeare to compose this play, but whatever darkness drove him to it was not something to which audiences responded well. The play tells the story of an elderly king, whose decision to divide his kingdom among his daughters opens the gates of hell upon his land, leading to death and despair for nearly all concerned.

I portrayed Cordelia, Lear's youngest daughter, the only one who is brave enough to tell him the truth. And for doing so, by play's end, she pays with her life.

In the last moments of the play, the darkest of which I ever performed, Burbage, who played my father, Lear, carried my dead body on stage. His lines were truly heartbreaking:

> And my poor fool is hanged, No, no, no life.
> Why should a dog, a horse, a rat have life,
> And thou no life at all? O thou wilt come no more.
> Never, never, never, never, never. Pray you, undo
> This button. Thank you, sir.

At which point, written on the roll, were the simple sounds "O, O, O, O!" These were Master Shakespeare's cues to Burbage to let loose and to give it his all, to let the audience in the Globe understand his pain before speaking his last words. Standing over my, or Cordelia's, dead body, he in truth appeared to will his own death, saying, "Break heart, I prithee break."

The silence from the audience at play's end led us to understand that the play had, perhaps, been too much to bear, with too much pain, too much darkness. Unlike any other of Shakespeare's plays, the tragedy ended without giving the audience the slightest glimmer or hint of hope. They appeared to hate it, this being the first occasion I ever witnessed this when one of his plays was staged.

He never talked about the failure of *Lear*, in the same manner in which he never talked about the success of his other plays. And while he remained silent, I sensed from his demeanor and the look in his eyes after the first performance that the failure of the audience to respond and his failure to reach them hurt him a great deal.

Master Shakespeare later revised the play. He gave the "O, O, O, O!" to another actor, gave Lear's line asking that his heart break to the character Kent, and even granted the audience a hint of relief, not only allowing Lear's suffering to end, but giving him the grace of dying with the hope, deluded though it might be, that his beloved Cordelia is still alive:

> And my poor fool is hanged! No, no, no life?
> Why should a dog, a horse, a rat have life,
> And thou no breath at all? Thou'lt come no more,
> Never, never, never, never, never!
> Pray you undo this button. Thank you sir
> Do you see this? Look on her, look, her lips,
> Look there, look there!

I never had the opportunity to play Cordelia with the changes Shakespeare made, and it was an odd sensation to witness another actor personate the role I had originated. It was as if I was watching myself as someone else.

But even with the changes, the play, whose greatness I later came to appreciate, was seldom revived. It was the rare occasion in which Master Shakespeare failed to reach his audience.

And it is perhaps odd that the play did not do so, for within weeks of our first performance of Lear, the plague once again returned to ravage London, leading the entire city to a state of complete despair.

Chapter Sixteen

In which there is yet another outbreak of the plague, we perform *Macbeth* before King James and King Christian of Denmark, and I offer a brief look at my life off the stage

In July, the theaters were shut down because of the plague, forcing us once again to lower the flag at the Globe and lock our doors. In the outbreak of two years earlier, more than thirty thousand residents of London had lost their lives, forcing the Privy Council to order that all public playing would cease when deaths in the course of one week rose above thirty. In the summer of 1606, deaths reached a height of 116 during the last week of August before the disease, as it had so often before, ran its course with the return of colder weather.

This was one of many epidemics I witnessed during my life, and although, praise be to God, I was fortunate enough never to have fallen ill, I still remained fearful that like my brother William and many of my classmates at home and acquaintances in the city, I would fall victim.

It was a disease that could only have been sent by the Devil himself, for the suffering it caused its victims was beyond all human reckoning and, apparently, beyond the power of God himself to ease except unto death.

A fever of unimaginable intensity was the first sign that one had fallen ill. The sufferer's heartbeat became rapid, making it impossible to catch one's breath. Severe, even excruciating pain began in the back and legs, and the throat became parched and dry with a thirst impossible to quench. Some victims suffered from an inability to walk properly; others from great unrelenting pain in nearly every part of the body. Next there were eruptions of plague sores found around the victim's armpits, neck and groin. These sores often swelled up until they burst, causing such agonizing pain that victims with alarming regularity took their own lives rather than suffer any longer — a mortal sin for which, I pray, God would forgive them.

In the last days of the disease, it became impossible to speak normally, and because of constant pain and fever, the victims raved like lunatics or became delirious, before, finally and blessedly, their hearts gave out and their agonies came to a merciful end.

It is no wonder then that when the plague struck, panic-stricken residents of the city fled to the surrounding countryside, for not only was the disease itself to be dreaded, but during the worst days, if anyone in your house fell ill, everyone else in the house was held under quarantine along with them. A cross was painted on the doorway to warn others to stay away, while all residing there were forced to remain inside until the disease ran its course, or until, as was more often the case, all inside succumbed.

And although the days when the epidemics were at their worst appear to have come to an end, I shall never forget what those years were like — the moans and shrieks and screams of agony emanating from the houses under quarantine; the smell of death everywhere as bodies piled up too quickly to be disposed of by city authorities; and finally, the creaking wheels of the carts making their way slowly down the near-empty streets, piled high with corpses, with more added as the drivers of the carts (employed at a profession I cannot imagine myself doing even at the threat of death) cried out, "Bring down your dead."

We were fortunate to be out of London for the worst of it, with performances at Oxford and Leicester, at Marlborough and Dover and Maidstone, and, of primary importance, at Greenwich and Hampton Court before King James and his most honored guest, King Christian IV of Denmark.

We stayed several days at Greenwich, where King James spent what appeared to be a goodly fortune and then some in hosting King Christian, who was the brother of his wife, Queen Anne. Much to everyone's sorrow, she had recently suffered the loss of her newborn daughter, Sophia, who had during the previous month been interred at Westminster Abbey.

Even with the gloom and pall of Sophia's death hanging overhead, the festivities were of a kind, I was told, reminiscent of the descriptions of paradise common among Mohammedans. There were women of great beauty, and there were magnificent feasts.

On one occasion wines and liquors of the highest quality were so plentiful that even the ladies of the court abandoned their good sobriety and could be seen rolling about on the ground in a state of utter intoxication, much to the amusement of King Christian, as well as the seeming dismay of King James, who, it must be said, did not appear to enjoy the festivities as much as did the others.

On one such evening, after our afternoon's performance of *Hamlet*, in which I personated Ophelia, presenting a tragedy about the prince of Denmark in front of the current king of Denmark, we were invited to remain to watch the evening's entertainment. It was a masque that told the story of the Queen of Sheba, not so much through the use of language as with Master Shakespeare, but through poetry, song, costume and dance.

But alas, this performance ended in disaster due to the copious amounts of drinking by the masque's amateur performers. The lady who played the role of the Queen of Sheba, while carrying precious gifts to the two kings in the audience, miscounted the steps, or so it seemed, dropping the presents into the king of Denmark's lap before falling completely atop of him. Naturally there was much confusion and shouting for servants and napkins, and after His Majesty's clothing and person were put back in reasonable order, he rose to dance with the Queen of Sheba but himself fell down, caused, I was later told, by many hours of feasting and drinking. He was carried into the palace and laid on his bed, his garments, as a servant breathlessly told us later that night, still covered by the remains of the wine, cream, jelly, cakes and other goodly consumables that the queen had bestowed upon him. Despite his hasty departure from the festivities, the entertainment continued, even though the participants who were in a state of drunkenness outnumbered those who were not by an increasingly sizable amount.

And again, truth be told, our performance of *Macbeth* at Hampton Court in August, while I believe effective, was difficult for all of the performers since, once more, the members of the court had enjoyed a goodly amount of wine and strong spirits before the play began. The majority of the audience talked among themselves during the drama, and by the end of the play, the soft snores of His Majesty King James I could distinctly be heard during Burbage's final speeches.

By late October the plague had finally retreated in London, so after several months' touring, we returned home to begin work on new plays — plays that we would rehearse and perform at the Globe in preparation for our command performances for the king over the Christmas-Candlemas season.

I suggested at the opening of this chapter that I would begin to speak of my life off the stage. But, truth be told, during this period, I had no life apart from the theater. The hours working at the Globe were long, and I was playing different roles on stage as often as six days a week, leaving me no time of my own in which to explore London, to meet new people and to make new friends, or even, unfortunately, to spend time with friends I had already made.

On rare occasions, I would not be so exhausted at the end of the day that I would then go for supper at a nearby tavern with one or another of my fellow players at the Globe. On even rarer occasions, I would be able to spend time with Alexander, now the father of two, who while exhausted himself and still somewhat aggrieved that my roles were now exceeding his both in length and importance, would come with me to dine and drink. On those nights when his consumption of beer was high, as was more and more often the case, rather than make the longer journey to his own home, he would come with me to Heminges's where he would, as in our younger days, share my bed and hold me safe and warm in his arms.

Those nights were infrequent and grew even more so as Christmas approached. Despite the fact that my new role in Barnabe Barnes's *The Devil's Charter*, which related the story of the bloodthirsty Borgia family of Italy, was compared to roles I had previously undertaken relatively straightforward, it still involved a great deal of time to prepare.

As I read through and learned my role, it became evident that there were strong similarities between Lucrezia Borgia and Lady Macbeth, similarities that would help me in my portrayal. They begin early on when Lucrezia calls upon the spirits, as did the lady, to help her as she prepares not to kill the king, but her own husband, Gismond:

> You grisly daughters of grim Erebus,
> Which spit out vengeance from your viperous hairs,
> Infuse a three-fold vigour in these arms,
> Immarble more my strong, indurate heart,
> To consummate the plot of my revenge.

These lines lacked, I noted even then, the poetic subtlety that Master Shakespeare had imparted to the lady. But as an actor, I could see and appreciate how the more direct approach of Barnes, if spoken with the proper amount of unlady-like ferocity, might please and excite an audience in ways that Shakespeare could not.

And again, in what I saw as my best scene, when I, or Lucrezia as it were, stabs her husband in such a manner as to stir the emotions of the audience, while lacking Shakespeare's consummate artistry, there was for me, as an actor, an opportunity to shout and gesticulate straight upwards to the heavens. After placing my hand over my husband's mouth to prevent him from speaking or crying out for help, I pull out his dagger with a grand gesture and most kindly offer to gag him:

Peace, wretched villain! Then receive this quickly:
Or by the living powers of heaven I'll kill thee!

After gagging him, I was to take a piece of paper out of my bosom and order him to write the words that would let the world know that I was innocent of any sins I had previously been accused of, and that he had taken his life by his own hand. I was then to tell him with a flourish and as much bravado as I could muster that he would die by my hand alone, and while feverishly acting, stab him six times.

After much more evildoing, Lucrezia is herself poisoned, which again granted me the opportunity to play on the grandest scale imaginable. But I can now see clearly that the drama lacked what Shakespeare gave to *Macbeth* — poetry and artistry, along with the sense that the lady, for all her faults most grievous, was still human, something that Barnes was not able to or did not care to impart to Lucrezia.

I feel a foul stink in my nostrils;
Some stink is vehement and hurts my brain;
My cheeks both burn and sting. Give me my glass.
Out, out, for shame! I see the blood itself
Dispersed and inflame'd! Give me some water!
…
My brains intoxicate, my face is scalded!
Hence with the glass! Cool, cool my face! Rank poison
Is minister'd to bring me to my death!
I feel the venom boiling in my veins!
…
Who painted my fair face with these foul spots?
You see them in my soul, deformed blots!

Lines such as these, I must allow, were both easier to remember and easier to present to an audience than those of Shakespeare. Indeed, it was the lack of depth in Lucrezia's character that made it in some ways a relief to portray her. She lacked a complex character that I would need to understand fully in order to successfully personate her on stage, so I was able to rely solely on oratory, reading her lines as mere empty words. The acting advice Master Shakespeare had given me on the occasion of our first meeting was useless in playing Lucrezia; indeed, doing the opposite of what he taught would be the only way to play her. It was in some ways a respite to me as an actor to just, as it were, act.

However, I must also allow that the challenge of playing Shakespeare's characters stirred something in me that personating Barnes's characters did not. Working to understand Shakespeare's characters, and working on finding something within myself that would help me to understand and personate them, brought me the deepest satisfaction.

I was now, I say with some amount of pride, at the moment of my career in which playing a female role had become a simple matter of allowing myself to become female. The challenge now was in playing a female who was very different from myself.

The next role I took on, one written again with me in mind by Master Shakespeare, would be, I think, the most challenging I dared to undertake.

Chapter Seventeen

In which I am Cleopatra

Once again I was asked by Master Shakespeare to attend to him at his lodgings. There I found him in his usual attire. His desk was again covered with papers encircled by books, and one, Plutarch's *Lives of the Noble Greeks and Romans*, the volume of *Parallel Lives* I'd noted on my first visit, was open to a chapter entitled "Life of Antony." Tybalt was happily purring next to the hearth.

"I have nearly completed what I hope will be our next new play, *The Tragedy of Antony and Cleopatra*. There is still some work to be done with it, but I plan on finishing within the next week, time permitting. But before I continue, I need enquire of you, do you think you are up to the challenge of performing Cleopatra? The role will be, when all is said and done, the longest you've played for me by far, as well as, I strongly suspect, the most difficult. But if you play it as I know you are capable of so doing, it will be the role that will make your name throughout London.

"But first let me ask you this, John. What do you know of Cleopatra?"

I spent a moment summoning up what I had learned in primary school, during what seemed like an earlier life, before telling him that I knew she had been the queen of Egypt; that she was known for her beauty and her ability to use that beauty to win first the heart of Julius Caesar, with whom she had borne a son, and then after Caesar's death, the heart of Marc Antony, whom she made her next lover, luring him away from his responsibilities in Rome. And then after their military defeat at (and I confess I struggled to remember the name of the battle of Actium) Antony and Cleopatra killed themselves.

"Very good," Shakespeare said. "Your education has served you well. What I hope to achieve is a character who goes beyond the common perception of Cleopatra as simply a female seductress who used her beauty to bend the will of men to gain her own ends. I want to bring out all of her character, all of her infinite variety, and turn Plutarch's prose story into one of poetry and, dare I say, magic.

"Look more closely, Master Rice," he told me, "at my copy of Plutarch. It should be open to the description of Cleopatra arriving by barge to meet Antony for the first time. Would you read it aloud for me?"

She herself reclined beneath a canopy spangled with gold, adorned like Venus in a painting, while boys like Loves in paintings stood on either side and fanned her. Likewise also the fairest of her serving-maidens, attired like Nereïds and Graces, were stationed, some at the rudder-sweeps, and others at the reefing-ropes.

Wondrous odours from countless incense-offerings
diffused themselves along the river-banks. Of the
inhabitants, some accompanied her on either bank
of the river from its very mouth, while others went
down from the city to behold the sight.

"I admire Plutarch greatly," Shakespeare told me, "but I
took it upon myself to make —" and here he smiled knowingly at me, "assorted improvements. Let me read this to
you if you will:

> The barge she sat in, like a burnished throne
> Burned on the water; the poop was beaten gold;
> Purple the sails, and so perfumed that
> The winds were love-sick with them; the oars were
>   silver,
> Which to the tune of flutes kept stroke, and made
> The water which they beat to follow faster,
> As amorous of their strokes. For her own person,
> It beggared all description; she did lie
> In her pavilion, cloth-of-gold of tissue,
> O'erpicturing that Venus where we see
> The fancy outwork nature. On each side her
> Stood pretty dimpled boys, like smiling cupids,
> With divers-coloured fans, whose wind did seem
> To glow the delicate cheeks which they did cool,
> And what they undid did.

"A few changes here and there, John, made, I think, all
the difference. Look," he said, as eager as a proud schoolboy to show me what he had done, "look at just the first

line. Where Plutarch wrote, 'in a barge with gilded poop,' I wrote:

The barge she sat in, like a burnished throne
Burned on the water. The poop was beaten gold …

"Can you hear the difference, John? And of greater importance, when you envision the scene, do you see the difference? Whereas Plutarch, a great historian, mind you, gave a mere description, what I did was add reaction. Where he wrote about the golden poop and the purple sails, I added 'and so perfumed that / The winds were love-sick with them.' That is what I have strived to do throughout the play, to create, I hope … poetry."

Here he stopped somewhat shamefacedly to ask me, "You will keep this secret between us, will you not, John? It wouldn't do if the rest of the men knew how simple it is for me to create."

And then, with a cough, he continued.

"That scene, my beautiful Cleopatra, is what I would like for you to bear in mind when reading the play, and then later while acting it. See in your mind the beauty of the queen, your beauty, John, making such a grand appearance that the winds themselves are love-sick for you. Plutarch describes you as being 'adorned like Venus in a painting.' I want you to see yourself and for our audiences to see you not just dressed as Venus, but indeed as Venus, the goddess of love herself. Do you think you're capable of doing that, John?"

I nodded, although I was not entirely confident that I was capable of doing, of being what he asked.

"Good. Now, I think you're ready to learn to become Cleopatra in a different manner than we have before. I am not going to lead you through your lines, at least not at first. What I want you to do is take this." Here he handed me another copy of the manuscript that he had had prepared for me especially. "And read it well. Come back to me in three days and tell me how you see Cleopatra and what you think you need do to bring her to life.

"Just one more word from me, John, before I send you on your way. Your responsibility, your job as an actor, is to make Cleopatra a tragic heroine. She is blamed, and rightfully so I would say, for the destruction of Marc Antony. But — and this is going to be crucial to the play — you must make clear to the audience that her final act, that of taking her own life, is one of such bravery and courage and nobility that they will see her as a heroine, perhaps of equal greatness to the noble Antony himself.

"Now, go read and study your lines, and return hence in three days."

So between performances and rehearsals, before arriving at the Globe and then after returning to my room, I read the play over and over again, learning the lines, trying to envision myself as Cleopatra, thinking about how I might move and speak and gesture and change myself from a sixteen-year-old English boy into a thirty-nine-year-old Egyptian queen. What in me was in her? How could I make an audience believe that I was not John Rice, or at least forget that I was John Rice on the stage, and was instead Cleopatra?

Shakespeare was correct when he told me that this role would be the most difficult one I had ever been given. While I had proved myself in earlier roles, I had increasing doubts that I would be able to do this one, and considered for a moment asking him if one of the other boy actors might perhaps be a better choice. But I also knew, the more I read and learned my role, that if I did not dare to become Cleopatra, if I did not screw my courage to the sticking place, I would disappoint Masters Shakespeare and Heminges. And so on returning to discuss the role with her creator, I boldly announced that I was ready.

"John, that is most excellent news. While writing it, I could not and still cannot imagine any other boy actor but you capable of portraying my Cleopatra. Burbage will of course portray Antony. As with you, I cannot imagine anyone other than him in the role, and along with that, you do work well with him. Also, I thought Alexander Cook might portray your maidservant, Iras — the two of you were friends as I recall. So let me ask you, my young thespian, what are your thoughts on the role? Do you have any questions?"

I could feel my face turn white, then red when Shakespeare mentioned my beloved Alexander, who had once played only leading roles but would now be featured in a small role as my servant. The news was unsettling, and while I felt for Alexander and wondered how it might affect our friendship, it reminded me that I was now the age that he had been when he was assigned the best roles of our repertory. Within a few years at best, I would be where Alexander was now, playing in support of a new boy actor.

And that is when I realized how it was that I was Cleopatra.

I told Master Shakespeare that I now, at least in part, understood the role. It was true of her, as he wrote, that

Age cannot wither her, nor custom stale
Her infinite variety.

Her nature, as portrayed in the play, was constantly shifting, indeed of infinite variety. Her passions, her anger, her wit, her constantly shifting temperament were all part of what kept Antony by her side. An ordinary woman such as his Roman wife, Octavia, would never satisfy him, and Cleopatra knew this and played upon him like an actress to ensure that he was entertained and in her thrall.

But, I said, thinking of Alexander and then myself, underlying all that variety was her fear of aging. Her fear of losing her beauty and her allure, her fear of losing Antony to a younger, prettier rival, her fear of no longer being the Cleopatra she thought she was. Age, contrary to the play's earlier words, would indeed wither her as it does us all. As, I realized, but dared not say aloud, it would me, as it had started to do with Alexander.

I stood waiting for Shakespeare's response. He sat silently for a moment as though pondering my words, and said only, "I chose my Cleopatra well."

He continued then, with a bemused look on his face, and asked, "Did you enjoy my little joke about boy actors, John? Remember the moment when, fearful that she will be taken to Rome as Emperor Octavian's prisoner and put on display, she tells her servants:

… 'tis most certain Iras. Saucy lictors
Will catch at us like strumpets, and scald rhymers
Ballad us out o'tune. The quick comedians

Extemporally will stage us and present
Our Alexandrian revels; Antony
Shall be brought drunken forth; and I shall see
Some squeaking Cleopatra boy my greatness
I' th' posture of a whore.

He observed, I am certain, the worried look on my face. He always knew, it seemed, what I was thinking and feeling before I myself did.

"Do not think, John, that the audience will laugh at you as part of the joke. Yes, it is true that you are a squeaking Cleopatra boy — the kind of actor that Cleopatra is fearful of being forced to watch portray her in a Roman revel of some sort — but fear not. Say the words as Cleopatra would and you will take the audience with you, from the reality of watching actors in their roles to viewing you as Cleopatra herself. Forget, at least for a time, that you are a boy actor yourself. Played as I know you can do it, you will be Cleopatra and only Cleopatra. Please, John, trust me. This will play just as I tell you it will."

And while I did trust Master Shakespeare with all my heart, that still did not stop me from worrying about my ability to do justice to the role and all the toil he had put into it.

Given the inherent difficulties of my role as well as Burbage's, in addition to the sheer complexity of the drama, with one scene unfolding into another as Shakespeare seemingly included the entire world on the stage, our rehearsal time was extended an extra day. But still, I was not at all certain that I would be successful.

Would I be able to be a convincing Cleopatra with just the barest of sets and with costuming that, until the last moments of the play and unlike the masques I'd seen performed before King James, did little to tell the audience that I was an Egyptian queen? I would have to rely solely on makeup to indicate my difference from Antony, along with my voice, gestures, movements and all that I had learned over the course of my apprenticeship to make Cleopatra a believable breathing personage; to force the audience to forget, at least in part, that they were at the Globe watching an actor, and a boy actor at that; to make them believe they were watching Cleopatra in Egypt. As I was able to convince myself as well as the audience that I was an Egyptian queen, so too would the audience need to be convinced that what they were seeing was real.

And I believe in that, I and we were successful.

I felt at ease and comfortable throughout the majority of the play. I was able to work with Burbage and the others, including Alexander, to showcase Cleopatra and her "infinite variety"; her flirtations with and love for Antony; her rage and jealousy and fear of aging on learning that Antony, who had been called back to Rome, had married the sister of the Emperor Octavian; her overwhelming need for reassurance that his new wife did not rival her, or me, in looks; her happiness on his return to Egypt and her bed; the disastrous defeat at sea, which she in part caused at the battle of Actium; Antony's suicide, which Burbage enacted most beautifully; and finally her captivity, awaiting news of her fate at the hands of the victorious Octavian.

It was at that point though, that I felt my self-confidence desert me. The play's last moments, for the most part, relied solely on myself to make them work, with some assistance from the actor portraying the Roman Dolabella and my dear Alexander. I could see that despite his discomfort and, I believe, a hint of jealousy, he could still look at me and with one glance make it clear that he still loved me and had nothing but faith in me and my ability.

So with that knowledge, I was able to go forth. I took a large and unfortunately audible breath for which I knew Heminges would berate me afterwards, and addressing the Roman Dolabella, Caesar's representative, spoke of my love and extreme feelings of loss for Antony:

> I dreamt there was an emperor Antony.
> O, such another sleep, that I might see
> But such another man!
> …
> His face was as the heavens, and therein stuck
> A sun and moon which kept their course and lighted
> The little O, the earth.
> …
> His legs bestrid the ocean; his reared arm
> Created the world; his voice was propertied
> As all the tuned spheres, and that to friends;
> But when he meant to quail and shake the orb,
> He was as rattling thunder. For his bounty,
> There was no winter in't; an autumn it was
> That grew the more by reaping. His delights
> Were dolphin-like: they showed his back above
> The element they lived in. In his livery
> Walked crowns and crownets; and islands were
> As plates dropped from his pocket.

My mood, Cleopatra's mood, our mood here was mournful and at the same time hopeful, needing to hear from another that Antony's greatness was of that scale. I asked Dolabella:

Think you there was or might be such a man
As this I dreamt of?

But his reply was a simple and truthful, "Gentle madam, no."

This gave me an opportunity to display and portray Cleopatra's rapidly shifting moods, her ability to confound her audience, as she raged, "You lie up to the hearing of the gods!"

Then came the moment I had expressed concern about to Master Shakespeare, as Cleopatra seemingly makes reference to me:

… 'tis most certain Iras. Saucy lictors
Will catch at us like strumpets, and scald rhymers
Ballad us out o'tune. The quick comedians
Extemporally will stage us and present
Our Alexandrian revels; Antony
Shall be brought drunken forth; and I shall see
Some squeaking Cleopatra boy my greatness
I' th' posture of a whore.

And while I heard one of the minor players behind me whisper to another calling me Alexander's whore, from the audience the reaction was as Shakespeare had promised me. I had taken them with me, and to them I was Cleopatra. My confidence grew as Cleopatra's greatness grew, as she prepared herself for death and a promised reunion with her beloved Antony:

> Give me my robe. Put on my crown. I have
> Immortal longings in me.

Feeling Alexander's strong hands on me, draping my purple robe around my shoulders, placing the crown on my head, I felt fully Cleopatra as well, ready and willing to die. Shoulders back and head held high in royal splendor, I felt in complete control of the role, of the play, of myself and of the audience. I was no longer John Rice — I had gone beyond that. For a moment or two, I entirely lost myself. I was Cleopatra.

Moments later, I placed the asp, the poisonous snake of the Nile, to my bosom, and in words very unlike Lady Macbeth's confessed willingness to tear the babe from her breast, I said,

> Dost thou not see my baby at my breast
> That sucks the nurse to sleep?

And, as beautifully and as regally as I was able to do, I slowly died, remaining as I did and as much as it was within my power to do so, every inch a queen. The audience, to my extreme satisfaction, fell into a hushed silence, as did Cleopatra herself. I had won.

Chapter Eighteen

In which we spend Christmas
at Whitehall, I am greeted by
His Royal Highness, James I,
and I am confronted with my
future

During the course of our appearances at Whitehall over the holiday season of 1606 and 1607, commencing on St. Stephen's Night, the day following the commemoration of the birth of our Savior, through Candlemas, until our final performance on the 27th of February, we performed nine plays. In four of them I was featured as the female lead, and in two, I was asked to double in an additional role.

On St. Stephen's Night, we performed *King Lear*. In addition to my role as Cordelia, I was asked, due to the unexpected illness of Robert Armin, to personate the Fool, who appears shortly after Cordelia's banishment to France and disappears from the play, for reasons Master Shakespeare never explains, shortly before her return.

It was my first opportunity to play the Fool, who much like Cordelia is the only person brave enough to tell Lear the truth about who he is. Burbage was a magnificent Lear, and I took full advantage of doing our scenes together. The Fool and Lear have several conversations of great import, in which I was able, disguised by the Fool's nonsensical rhymes, to tell Lear things that he was in need of hearing.

I was also given the opportunity to sing nonsense songs, which again masked truths, to cavort and in general do all in my power to amuse and distract the king from his growing madness.

It was a role unlike any I had ever had and ever would have again, given Armin's near monopoly on such comic clowns. So taking advantage of the opportunity to perform before the royal court, playing both Cordelia, a royal daughter and queen of France, as well as the young boy that was the Fool, I somehow became both. Going from one to the other and back again was an exhilarating and exhausting experience, one I was glad to have had, and perhaps equally glad to not have to do again, at least not with any frequency.

After the performance had ended and the jig had been danced, Burbage and I, along with several of the other actors, were summoned to receive thanks from our patron, King James, even though His Royal Highness and court, much like the audience at the Globe, did not appear to know exactly what to make of the drama they had witnessed.

It was my first encounter with King James, although as I have noted, I had witnessed his greeting to Alexander on several previous occasions. This time though, it was me whom he wanted to meet.

I was in Cordelia's dress when, on being presented to him, I politely curtsied and put out my hand. The king kissed it, and then pulling me closer as I had seen him do with Alexander, he allowed his hand to brush against my arse while at the same time he whispered in my ear to inform me that he had been watching me over the last few seasons and was pleased to note what he called my progress. Calling a servant bearing a silver tray to his side, he removed a small box from the tray. As he pressed the box into my hand, he told me that there would be more to follow, before sending me forward and moving on to Burbage.

The king's actions, while not entirely unexpected, were all the same frightening, even distasteful given the king's general appearance, but also, I must allow, flattering. I looked back at Alexander. He stared at me with an unreadable look on his face before giving me a wink and an odd smile. Apparently, it seemed, this would be something between myself and the king — something that he appeared not willing to assist me with, although it was equally apparent that he was amused to see me follow along his path. Upon my return home, when I opened the box the king had given me, I found a beautiful gold ring.

Nine days later, on the 8th of January, we presented *Macbeth*, hoping that with the absence of Christian IV of Denmark, the court might pay attention to the play itself rather than drinking and gossiping among themselves throughout the performance. They did, and because they did, they were fortunate enough to witness Burbage give what I think was the finest and strongest performance I ever saw. It took all I had to stay with him as he transformed himself into Macbeth, to match his force with mine and to believably be the lady who pushes him to murder to achieve his, or actually, their goals. It was exhilarating to find myself pushed by Burbage beyond what I thought I was capable of. And once again, the court responded as well as any of us could have hoped.

In addition, I was commanded by the king to appear before him once again, this time as the lady. I curtsied as gracefully as possible and was again rewarded — if one could indeed call it a reward — by being drawn closer to His Majesty, while his hand seemed to caress rather than graze my buttocks, after which an exquisite bracelet was pressed into my hand.

On this occasion, when I looked over towards Alexander, he had a smile on his face, as if seeming to sense and even enjoy my slight discomfort. Whether he was taking what appeared to be a prurient interest in watching someone else touching me where he alone had previously done so, I know not. Soon after, he watched me closely as I transformed from Lady Macbeth back to John Rice, whispering to me that if I continued to allow the king to take liberties with me, I would be, as he had been, rewarded handsomely.

Weeks later, on the 2nd of February, we were called back to Whitehall to perform *The Devil's Charter*. I thought our performance had been effective, but while the drama had been seen as a great success at the Globe, here at Whitehall in front of the royal court, it did not seem to have the same effect. Before the play had even finished, Queen Anne rose from her seat and left the hall. The rest of the court, including King James, seemingly taking their cues from her, began to take their leave as well, until only a few remained to attend through to the end.

Needless to say, we never performed *The Devil's Charter* in court again.

And given the reaction Barnes's play had received, we felt it incumbent upon us to remind the court that we were chosen by His Royal Highness to be the King's Men for a reason, and performing *Antony and Cleopatra* several days later, every actor played to their very best ability. It was, I'm pleased to be able to say, a performance that I suspect will live on in the memory of those in attendance.

I was again summoned to speak with the king and accept his favors. I curtsied in my royal robe, and again His Highness drew me closer. This time though, instead of his hand on my buttocks, I felt it on my member, which now that I was approaching adulthood stirred and swelled in response. The king looked at me in amused surprise as though until that moment he had been uncertain whether I was indeed male or female. He again whispered in my ear, this time asking me if I would be interested in joining him in his chambers later for a private audience, and then called over the servant with the silver tray and presented me with a beautiful gold brooch to display, not on my women's gowns, but on my leather jerkin.

I thanked His Majesty, but uncertain how to respond to his invitation, and now knowing exactly what was expected, moved away as quickly as possible, leaving him to address Burbage who, as even I well knew, was far too old to receive the king's gifts and invitations.

Later, when I spoke with Alexander about the invitation from the king, he at first seemed slightly jealous and then amused. He expressed disbelief that I had not accepted the invitation, telling me that he had on several occasions gone to the royal chambers to receive the king's favors and had been, as he had assured me earlier, handsomely rewarded for his pains.

I was, I confess, briefly taken aback that at the same time Alexander had been sharing a bed with me he was also, even if only on a few occasions, sharing a bedchamber with the king. I remember each of the nights he had been away, him telling me on his return that he had been out drinking with friends, and it being late had slept at their homes rather than make the journey back to Master Heminges's. And though I did feel a brief pang of jealousy, as well as disappointment in Alexander for not telling me the truth, I also appreciated his tact and sensitivity in not being completely open. Knowing me as well as he did, he knew that I would have been hurt beyond all measure, while at the same time not fully understanding why he was doing what he was doing.

Like Alexander, I was beginning to come to terms with the reality of my situation. I was now sixteen years old, my manhood had begun to make itself evident, the days when I would be able to persuasively be the lady, be Cleopatra, be a woman on stage who wasn't, like Alexander's Iras, an older character of lesser importance, were dwindling. I had two or three years at most before that would happen.

We were asked to give one final performance for the royal court before the season ended — a command performance of *As You Like It*, the first play I had seen before being apprenticed to the King's Men, just three and a half years earlier.

Only now it would be me, John Rice, who would play Rosalind. And Alexander, who had performed Rosalind so memorably in that first performance, would play Orlando, the young man who loves Rosalind and whom she loves in return. Alexander had been eighteen and at his peak as a boy actor when I had seen him. I was now the same age, and, I must humbly say, at my peak as well.

It was an unnerving experience for me, and, I suspect, for Alexander himself to have this on-stage role reversal, in addition to the role reversal in the play itself. As Rosalind, I would flee to the Forest of Arden dressed as the boy Ganymede and teach Alexander, as Orlando, how best to court and win the heart of Rosalind.

The performance played well. Perhaps the personal history between myself and Alexander served to heighten the romantic tension. At play's end, still in Rosalind's disguise as Ganymede, I stepped out to address the audience as Alexander had done in what seemed a previous existence:

If I were a woman I would kiss as many of you as had beards that pleased me, complexions that liked me and breaths that I defied not. And I am sure as many as have good beards, or good faces, or sweet breaths will for my kind offer, when I make curtsy, bid me farewell.

I felt the king's eyes on me and knew in an instant what would happen next.

And indeed he did summon me for an audience. He did, after I curtsied still dressed as the boy Ganymede, pull me closer, touch upon my member, speak well of me and give me a present. Once again, he invited me to visit him in his royal chambers, and with that, I had not only assumed Alexander's roles on stage, I was being asked to assume his role in the king's affections as well.

This time I accepted his invitation, as I did for the next two nights, during which time I learned two things. The king's clothing was very much padded to make him look larger than he was, as well as to protect against possible assassination. And despite the overwhelming odor of camphor in his chambers, each time I left I found myself crawling with lice — what His Royal Highness, for reasons I failed to understand, referred to as his "wee little ones" — which, because of the care I had always taken regarding my own personal cleanliness, I had up to now been fortunate to avoid.

But also, I must admit, Alexander was right. I was, for my pains, rewarded handsomely as well.

Chapter Nineteen

In which I attempt to explain
my reasons for visiting King
James in the royal chambers,
Ben Jonson comes to ask my
forgiveness, and I become, to
my regret, dissatisfied with the
King's Men

I confess that the occasions of my nighttime visits to the king's bedchambers are now among the greatest regrets of my life. It was a mistake to go — a mistake caused, at least in part, by a growing anxiety about losing my beauty along with a need to prove myself Alexander's equal. I had a mad belief that by doing so, I would be placing myself under the personal protection of the king who could then take an interest in me and lend me assistance if necessary.

The king, however, thought differently about the matter. After our third evening and his final gift, I was never asked to return. I later heard through others that his eye had settled on a new courtier, followed by the next one and then, yes, the next one.

The result being that I felt sullied by my visits to the royal bedchamber and by my acceptance of gifts from the king for so doing. I had become, using the words I myself had said on stage, a "squeaking Cleopatra … I' th' posture of a whore."

And even though I understood that Alexander had made the same arrangement with His Highness, I felt that he would look at me differently, that I had somehow made dirty what we had between us.

For now though, it was still my good fortune to play the finest women's roles available. No new plays by Master Shakespeare entered our repertory during that year. I suspect that having written *Macbeth*, *King Lear* as well as *Antony and Cleopatra* all within a period of a little more than a year, his pen had run, at least temporarily, dry.

I did play Katherine in a revival of his early comedy *The Taming of the Shrew*, which I must say was not a performance I was especially proud of. Broadly played farce of that sort was not, despite Master Heminges's insistence that I should take on the part, particularly suited to my temperament and stage demeanor. And while I acquitted myself without shame, it was not a role that I should have taken on. I knew myself, and whatever gifts I may have had on the stage did not include comic roles such as the shrew Katherine, as Master Shakespeare had told me years before.

My partial failure as Katherine aside, both Masters Heminges and Shakespeare, whose approval was all that mattered to me, seemed pleased with my work. But in addition to that, I received words of praise from a most unexpected source — Ben Jonson.

I had not spoken with and had, in fact, shied away from him ever since the day his cruel words had driven me off the stage in tears. But on this occasion, he came to me, searching me out as I was getting fitted for a costume, and, asking the tire man to leave us alone for a moment, he said, "I erred in my judgment of you, John, for which I humbly beg your pardon. I was wrong. You have proved yourself to be a player of much excellent skill and refinement, and I ask if you would do me the honor of performing in a small masque I have written for the Merchant Taylors' Company."

It was an odd and unexpected moment of triumph. Jonson had come to me to ask my forgiveness, and further for me to perform in a specially commissioned masque he had just composed. It was a moment of, dare I say, vindication?

And so it came to be that on the 16th of July 1607, I played a role of great prominence when the Merchant Taylors' Company, known as the Worshipful Company of Merchant Taylors, entertained His Majesty King James I at its guildhall in the City of London. Given that this was not a performance of the King's Men but a masque, it entailed elaborate sets and stage props and costumes, including a ship that was lowered from the rafters with three musicians on board dressed as mariners, who sang three songs written by Jonson.

For my role in the masque, I had the rare good fortune to wear an elaborate and beautiful costume befitting my appearance as an angel of light, carrying a taper of frankincense in a hand that no longer trembled while performing. Before the ship was lowered, I read a short but, I must allow, well-written speech of a mere eighteen lines — in all truth, a simple matter to learn when compared to what I had recently undertaken. The verse was composed especially for the occasion by Jonson. The audience seemed to well appreciate both the costumes and poetry, and Jonson himself told me afterwards that I had read his lines beautifully.

For our efforts, the Taylors' Company made record, later shared with Jonson and my Master Heminges, discussing the terms of payment:

> To Mr. Heminges for his direction of his boy that made the speech to His Majesty, forty shillings, and five shillings given to John Rice, the speaker.

This might be a good point in my narrative to note that several years later, I, along with Burbage, was asked to perform at a riverside pageant in honor of the investiture of the Prince of Wales in a drama written by Anthony Munday entitled *London's Love to Prince Henry*. Burbage appeared as the water king, Amphion, while I was his queen, Corinea.

Again, some time later, I was allowed to view the state disbursement records for the occasion:

> It is ordered that Mr. Chamberlain shall pay unto Mr. Burbage and John Rice, the players that rode upon the two fishes at the meeting of the high and mighty prince, the Prince of Wales, upon the River of Thames on Thursday last, seventeen pounds, ten shillings and six pence, by them disbursed for robes and other furniture for adorning themselves at the same meeting. And that they shall retain to their own use, in lieu

of their pains there taken, such taffeta, silk and other necessities as were provided for that purpose, without any further allowance.

It was later revealed to me that a spectator had said this about the performance, in words that somehow made their way to myself and Burbage, kindly referring to us as

… two absolute actors, even the very best our instant time can yield … Richard Burbage the Father of Harmony or Music … a grave and judicious prophetlike personate, attired in his apt habits every answerable to his state and profession, with his wreath of sea shells on his head and his harp hanging in fair twine before him … and John Rice was a very fair and beautiful nymph representing the genius of old Corineus' queen and the province of Cornwall's, suited in her watery habit yet rich and costly, with a coronet of pearls and cockle shells on her head.

In the course of the next several years, the roles I was given at the Globe slowly began to change. I was growing beyond the age when I could believably play a young woman, and the roles I was assigned changed accordingly.

In Shakespeare's *The Tragedy of Coriolanus*, a drama with, it must be said, fairly limited roles for women, I portrayed Volumnia, the mother of the tragic hero Caius Martius Coriolanus. In a manner very much like Lady Macbeth, she pushes and bends the ambitions of her son entirely to her own end, and with equally tragic results. Even more bloodthirsty, if possible, than the lady, she takes unseemly delight at the thought of pain, blood and honorable death. It was a role I very much enjoyed testing myself and my abilities with, though I was, perhaps, still too young to take on the role given that Burbage was portraying my son, Coriolanus. But as it was a relatively small role, that minor flaw in casting did not, I think, detract from the power of the play nor, I daresay, my performance.

I appeared in other plays as well — works by Shakespeare and others, including at last those of Jonson — but it seemed as though after portraying Lady Macbeth, Lucrezia Borgia, Cordelia, the Fool and Cleopatra in such a brief period of time, something was missing. I knew not whether it was in me and my realization of what time and age do, or whether is was Alexander's increasing absence from my life and bed as his family grew and his time for our friendship became more precious. Or indeed, perhaps it was the changing focus of Master Shakespeare's plays, from the roles in which I had achieved some level of renown to the roles in his new plays, which instead of focusing on powerful women focused on relationships lost and renewed between fathers and daughters in plays such as *The Winter's Tale* and *Cymbeline*.

These more elaborately produced dramas were performed at our new indoor theater, Blackfriars, which, in addition to the Globe, allowed us to perform year round. And while they involved roles I played to the best of my abilities and received much praise for, I still felt myself at a distance from them. I was no longer Rosalind or Cleopatra. I was, instead, John Rice playing those roles, a difference that the audience might not have been aware of but I was, as was, I suspect, Shakespeare himself.

There was another occurrence during this period that affected me deeply, one that I knew was inevitable but that I dreaded nonetheless. Heminges took on a new apprentice, a beautiful boy with the name of George Birche.

Young George was slender and blond, with long curls that set off his high-cheekboned innocence. I sensed his nervousness and excitement, which reminded me of my own when I first arrived in London in what seemed like a lifetime past. Master Heminges pulled me aside to ask if I would watch over him, and so, as Alexander had done with me, I became his protector, helping him adjust to his new life in London as an apprenticed boy actor, sharing my bed with him, and in time, as we became good friends, holding him tight at night.

It was an odd yet comforting feeling, one that helped to bring me closer to understanding Alexander and his experience when I first came to London. I knew, as Alexander did, that the beautiful boy sharing my bed, now actually sharing my life, would all too soon be my replacement on stage. He would be given the kinds of roles it had been my privilege to play but that I was rapidly, all too rapidly, outgrowing. And yet because of my love and appreciation for Alexander's ungrudging generosity and love towards me, I found it impossible to resent George. His beauty and innocence did not allow for that, and at night in bed, talking before sleep overcame us and feeling his warm body pressed tightly against mine, I knew that I would do for him and give to him all that Alexander had done for and given to me.

George was with us when, in 1610, the King's Men traveled to Oxford to perform an earlier work by Master

Shakespeare, *The Tragedy of Othello*, in which Burbage portrayed the African military hero himself. I had the chance to personate a role I had long wanted to attempt, that of Desdemona, the willful Venetian girl who loves Othello but is murdered by him in their wedding bed when he is driven mad with jealousy by the lies of his supposed friend Iago.

The performance had nearly reached its conclusion when Othello, believing the worst of his beloved Desdemona, informs her that she is to die, that she must die. Pleading for her life, she desperately cries out, "O, banish me lord, but kill me not!"

And it was then that the worst happened. My voice cracked, as all male voices must eventually do, signaling to all in attendance, including Burbage, whose face momentarily broke into an amused yet concerned look, that indeed my days as a boy actor were coming to an end.

I was fortunate in that I was able to hide my shame, for four lines later Desdemona is smothered by her husband and lord with a pillow. The remainder of the scene was spent silently dead, which happily seemed to earn the praise of one member of the audience who, as I was later told, reported that "Although she always acted her whole part extremely well, yet when she was killed she was even more moving, for when she fell back on the bed she implored the pity of the spectators by her very face."

It was interesting, I thought, that even with the cracking of my voice, the audience member made mention of me as "she."

Even with that kind of praise, I knew the time had come for a change. The King's Men had been good to me and had taught me my craft well, but if I remained I would forever be seen among my fellow actors and by the audience at the Globe as a boy actor gone beyond his years. So when my apprenticeship came to an end several months after *Othello*, I took a chance and opportunity to move on and work with actors who would, I hoped, see me in ways the King's Men could not or perhaps would not.

It was, as it turned out, an error most grievous.

Chapter Twenty

In which I leave the King's
Men but soon return, and
receive sad news, both
professional and personal

As my seven-year apprenticeship came to an end, I received
word from the newly forming Lady Elizabeth's Men asking
if I would be interested in joining them as one of the found-
ing members. I spoke with Heminges, who advised me in
his dual role as master and friend that I would do myself
better service by remaining with the troupe, but he would
also, if I so wished, give me blessing to leave if I thought
it would be in my best interest. I would have spoken with
Master Shakespeare regarding this matter as well, but he
was now spending the majority of his time away from the
Globe and London, at home in Stratford. He had been gaining
weight, and, I had taken note, was starting to display signs
of weariness and age.

And so with Heminges's reluctant blessing, I left the King's Men, and while still taking lodging with him and sharing a bed with George, although now as a paying renter, I joined the Lady Elizabeth's Men.

The newly bonded company was made up largely of aging boy actors like myself, many from the once popular troupes such as the Children of the Chapel and the Children of Paul's, both of which had lost much of their company to the plague.

Problems befell us from the start, largely in regards to theater space, and so we spent much of our time those first two years touring the countryside. Finally, in 1612, we were in London and had been invited to perform before the court. The plays we presented, which included Beaumont and Fletcher's *The Honest Man's Fortune* and Thomas Middleton's *A Chaste Maid in Cheapside*, were entertainments, but having been spoiled by my good fortune of acting in plays written by Master Shakespeare, they were not nearly as interesting or as challenging for me to perform. And I was certain they were not as entertaining or challenging for audiences either.

Even with limited royal support, we continued to struggle, and so it was that in 1613 we combined with the Children of the Queen's Revels, who performed at Whitefriars. Together we performed *A Chaste Maid in Cheapside* at the Swan in early 1613. We then combined with Prince Charles's Men later that same year, but by then I had largely had enough.

It felt like I had failed personally. I had struck out on my own, leaving the safety and security and camaraderie I had found with the King's Men, and instead found loneliness, struggle and roles in plays that, even though I was no longer a boy actor as such, I felt were not worthy of my time or that of the audience. And also, I confess, during this time I stained the purity of my feelings for Alexander as well as for George by indulging myself physically and lustfully with my fellow boy actors and various barmaids and the like I encountered while touring. These encounters, while satisfying my lustful nature, left me ultimately alone with my sins.

It was during this same time that the unthinkable happened — the Globe burned to the ground when a cannon fired at the beginning of Master Shakespeare's *All Is True* sent sparks flying up to the heavens. The thatched roof of the theater quickly started an inferno that burned my theatrical home to the ground in less than an hour.

There were, I am happy to note, no fatalities, thanks to the mercy of God. But as I was later told, there was one in the audience, whose name remains unknown, whose breeches caught on fire and would indeed have burned him alive, except for one quick-thinking gentleman, whose name also remains unknown, who emptied the contents of his bottle of ale on the hapless victim, putting out the flames.

And then, as if God were punishing me both for my sins and for abandoning the King's Men in search of greater personal glory, came — to my eternal and everlasting sorrow — the news that Alexander, my beloved friend and companion, died of fever in early 1614, leaving a wife and four children to mourn his memory.

He was gone. I had not had the chance to see him to say goodbye, and the grief I felt was entirely my own and has been with me since that day and will, I am certain, remain with me until the day I die. He was my first true friend, my protector, my first — and here I must confess and say for the first time directly and altogether accurately — my first and perhaps only real love.

With the loss of the Globe and of Alexander, I knew where it was I wanted to be — I needed to return home. I left Lady Elizabeth's Men and rejoined the King's Men, grateful to Heminges and the others that they would allow the prodigal son return.

My career since then has been one of steady if not spectacular success. I have played roles in *The Duchess of Malfi* and in *The Tragedy of Sir John van Olden Barnavelt*, where I portrayed both a captain and a servant, as well as in *The Spanish Viceroy*, sometimes playing female parts, other times the male. These roles, as well written as they were, did not match the excitement of playing the roles created by Master Shakespeare, who, as I've grown to appreciate and did not quite do so at the time, was a writer whose work went well beyond any one of his contemporaries.

That uniqueness became more readily apparent when word reached us in London that in April 1616, Master Shakespeare had died at home in Stratford, after, or so we were told, an evening spent drinking with Jonson and the poet Michael Drayton led to his contracting a fever from which he never recovered.

Master Shakespeare, who I am certain will be seen as the finest poet of his day, was buried at his local church in Stratford. None of the actors who knew him, worked with him and, yes, loved him, were in attendance. We held a small private wake in his honor on the stage of the Globe, the rebuilding of which was nearing completion. Each was asked to read a speech or work by Shakespeare in his honor. I chose a speech from a play that I had not had the opportunity to act in, *The Tempest*, one that I found profoundly moving, not only for its meaning within the play itself, but because, as I remembered well, Shakespeare had begun to conceive of it at the wedding party of my beloved friend, Alexander:

> Our revels now are ended. These our actors,
> As I foretold you, were all spirits and
> Are melted into air, into thin air;
> And — like the baseless fabric of this vision —
> The cloud-capped towers, the gorgeous palaces,
> The solemn temples, the great globe itself,
> Yes, all which it inherit, shall dissolve,
> And like this insubstantial pageant faded,
> Leave not a rack behind. We are such stuff
> As dreams are made on, and our little life
> Is rounded with a sleep.

Indeed, it seemed that our revels, with the passing of our friend and inspiration Shakespeare, had truly ended.

I continued working with my friends and fellow actors for nearly ten additional years, finally becoming a shareholder and officially entering the ranks of the King's Men with a livery allowance in the spring of 1621. During that time I played a variety of roles and continued to board at Heminges's, where I continued to share a bed with George until I followed in Alexander's path and married.

Her name was Lucy Abbott, the daughter of a wine merchant whose shop was near to the Globe. We would often exchange glances as I walked by deep in thought about whichever role I would be playing that day. Those glances grew to nods and greetings, until finally, Heminges, aware of what was taking place, took it upon himself to introduce me to Lucy and her father. And while Mr. Abbott was disappointed that I was a mere actor, the fact that I was with the King's Men was enough of an acknowledgment of royal favor that he agreed to allow us to court, and then, in due time, to marry.

Our marriage was a good one, although the feelings of closeness and friendship that I felt for Alexander were lacking. On the evenings I was unable to get home, I spent the night at Heminges's, sharing the bed with George for whom I grew to feel the same fondness that Alexander had undoubtedly felt for me. I would hold him close to keep ourselves warm, indulging in the same sort of activities Alexander had with me, and seemed, as time went on, to share my nights equally between him and Lucy.

It is here that I must share the sad news that within a year of our wedding, Lucy gave birth to a son, whom we named Alexander. However, as God willed it, both Lucy and our son were dead within days of his birth. I mourned her loss — although not to be compared to my love for Alexander, I did have feelings of fond friendship for Lucy, and I do still miss the time we had and her companionship.

Once again alone, I left our home and returned to living exclusively at Heminges's, where I paid for food and lodging, and shared a room and bed and affection with George, who seemed pleased that I had come back. But although he fully returned my friendship and affection, and he was in all respects a dear companion, he could not ever make up for all I had lost.

With the loss of Lucy and my dear Alexander, it seemed to me that I had lost my way. My acting had become rote and mechanical — I was reading my lines without meaning and my words without thought. My very existence itself seemed to be without meaning or purpose. I knew that my time as an actor was coming to an end.

On the 7th of May 1625, I, along with the rest of the King's Men, attended the funeral of King James I. Since with the death of His Royal Majesty we were no longer, as it were, the King's Men, it seemed an appropriate time to bring my life on the stage to an end.

For my new life, I intend, at last, to fulfill my mother's wish for me and devote myself to a God I have for too long not given sufficient attention to, committed as I have been to myself and my personal glory.

The time for that life, for my life as an actor and becoming persons that I am not, has come to an end.

An Ending and a Beginning

I was Cleopatra.

I was Lady Macbeth.

I was Cordelia in Master Shakespeare's *The Tragedy of King Lear*. And I was the Fool in the same play.

I was Imogen in *Cymbeline*. I was Marina in *Pericles*. I was Paulina in *The Winter's Tale*.

I was Desdemona when England's most renowned troupe of actors, the King's Men, performed in Oxford in 1610.

I was Lucrezia Borgia in Barnabe Barnes's *The Devil's Charter*.

I was summoned to perform on numerous occasions before King James I, his family and his court.

I was featured in plays written by William Shakespeare, Ben Jonson, John Webster and other leading playwrights of the time. I knew them, worked with them, learned from them and became, I like to think, their friends.

I was, for a time, an actor at the Globe Theatre in London, where before I entered my full adulthood and because of what some called my beauty — my physical qualities and appearance and demeanor — I was featured and praised for my performances in leading women's roles, to both my shame and, I must confess, my pride.

I was loved by boys and girls and by men and women. And I loved them in return.

My name is John Rice.

I am now thirty-five years old, childless, my dear beloved wife gone for nearly ten years. She died shortly after giving birth to our son, who followed her just three days later.

The theaters are closed because the plague is once again ravaging London. The time has now come to say goodbye to all of that. The time has come for me to turn my back on that world of fakery and artifice and make-believe, and return to the real world. The time has come for me to say goodbye to the theater and, if God wills it, to find a new life and salvation in the church.

Farewell then to that life.

AUTHOR'S NOTE

I Was Cleopatra is largely a work of my imagination.

John Rice did exist and was a boy actor at the Globe. The facts of his family, childhood and apprenticeship are unknown. Given the years that he was at the Globe with the King's Men, and the few times he appears in the historical records, it is possible to take an educated guess as to the roles he played, but they are suppositions.

His relationships with Masters Heminges and Shakespeare, his friendships with Alexander and George, the story of his first marriage to "Lucy" (her name is unknown) and his relationship with King James are, again, based on my own assumptions, knowing what is known about all those involved.

After leaving the King's Men, John Rice lived in the parish of St. Saviour's, Southwark, and joined St. Saviour's as a clerk in or around 1625. In 1630 he oversaw the will of Heminges, and in that same year, at the age of forty, he married Frances Legat and the couple proceeded to have six children over the course of the next eight years.

Frances died (although the date is not known), and John married Anne Westebrooke in 1644. He died ten years later, in 1654, and was buried in the church of Tarring Neville.

In his last will and testament, he described himself as "John Rice of Tarring Neville in the County of Sussex clerk being sick in body but of perfect memory."

When the first collected edition of the plays of William Shakespeare was published in 1623, assembled and edited by John Heminges and Henry Condell, it included a list under the heading "The Names of the Principal Featured Players in These Plays."

John Rice is one of only twenty-six actors on the list.

Dennis Abrams is the southern correspondent for *Publishers Weekly*. He has written more than thirty young adult biographies and history books. He is also the author of *The Play's the Thing*, a complete young adult guide to the plays of William Shakespeare. *I Was Cleopatra* is his first novel. He lives in Houston.